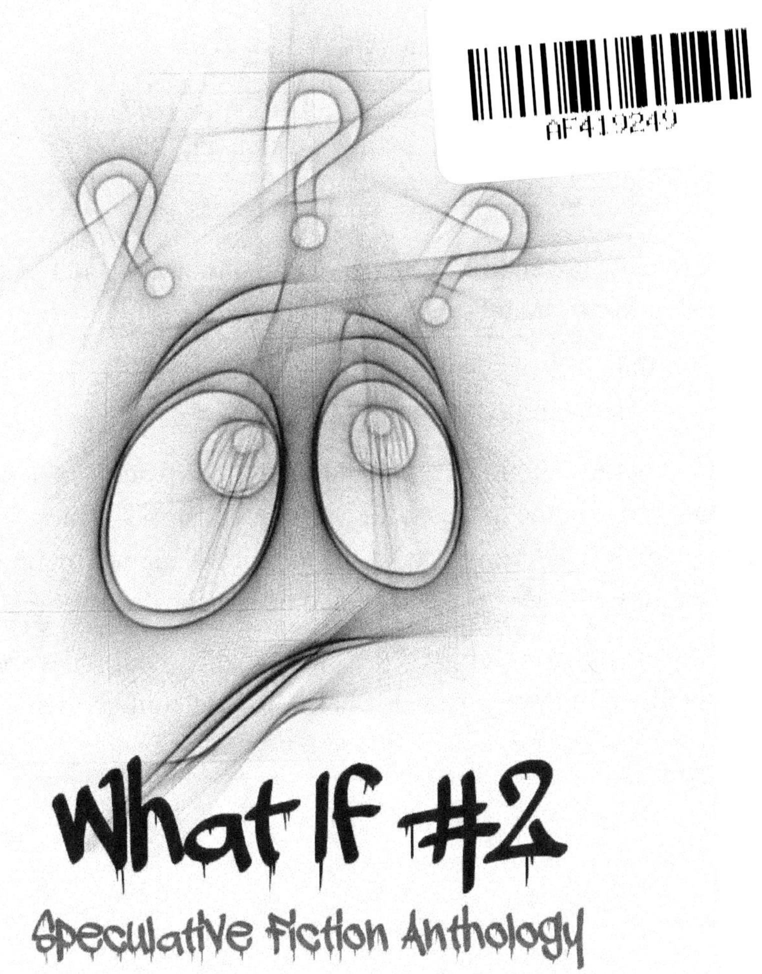

By GBBPub Authors:

Erika M Szabo, Lorraine Carey, Alan Zacher,
R.A. "Doc" Correa, David W. Thompson,
and Toi Thomas

Mysteries of the Wetland by Erika M Szabo and Lorraine Carey

Join Ava Jenson on vacation in her grandmother's old country when all mysterious events are connected to an ancient legend about a cursed church bell.

The Zanna by David W. Thompson

A potential stepmother and stepdaughter seek common ground at the family's rustic retreat. Will the past return to haunt them? Only Zanna knows...

Forbidden Love by Erika M Szabo

They knew their love was forbidden, but they couldn't help the way they felt. Their love for each other was too strong to ignore.

A Well-kept Home by Toi Thomas

Everyone knows how special the Fields Family Farm is. Some say it's haunted. Some say it's enchanted. But only those who dare to stay the night really know.

Don't Whistle Back by Erika M Szabo

Milena visits her grandfather in Mexico and wonders why he has a rope with seven knots tied to the door. She finds out soon enough!

J.A.C.K.S. by R. A. "Doc" Correa.

What is a human? According to the cybernetically enhanced officers of the U. S. Army's Joint Advanced Combat Knowledge System program, they are the only real humans.

She Decided to Be a Vampire by Erika M Szabo

Every kid in town knew that old Mrs. Robbins was a vampire. What they didn't know and are about to find out, will change their lives forever.

T'is Was The Night by Alan Zacher

This Christmas tale is about a family coming to "terms" with the alleged existence of Mo-Mo, aka, "The Missouri Monster"; aka, their own Bigfoot.

W.I.DG.E.T.S. by R. A. "Doc" Correa

The U. S. Army pursues the technologies "improving" Soldier-Machine Interface for Future Combat Systems. What are the consequences for humans?

The Unlucky Number Four by Erika M Szabo

In China, the number four sounds like the word death, making the number highly unlucky. Hua is the fourth child in her family.

Push by David W. Thompson

Leona is a missing mother and Sergeant James is on the hunt. When family secrets are revealed, he must find her, or it will be the cadaver dog's turn.

Bravery Has a Price by Erika M Szabo and Lorraine Carey

After boasting to her twin brothers that she is braver than they are, Emma immediately regrets it. Is proving her courage worth the price she must pay?

Mysteries of the Wetland

By Erika M Szabo and Lorraine Carry

Ava Jenson sighed as she glanced over the travel brochure for the impressive resort in Siofok, Hungary. Hotel Azur overlooking Lake Balaton with an elegant glass facade looked inviting. It had a spa, an outdoor café and a five-star restaurant. She'd always wanted to visit Hungary as her grandmother was born there and immigrated to the US as a young woman. Her stories always fascinated Ava, but her husband for ten long years had refused the idea of a European vacation and always bullied her into doing what he liked.

It'd been five years since her nasty divorce, and she was finally ready to venture out on her own. She hadn't had a vacation since then and with so much unused vacation time from her job at the boutique, she decided to make it a two-week stay.

Sipping her coffee, she remembered what the travel agent told her about Lake Balaton's clean water and the striking emerald-green color due to its chemical composition. It's heavy in carbonates and sulfates, and there are also around 2000 species of algae that grow in its waters. Ava phoned the travel agent; she'd made her payment and was all set to go at the end of the month.

The two weeks flew by fast, and after nine hours of an exhausting overnight flight, she arrived in Budapest. The two-hour taxi ride to Siofok was pleasant with the chatty driver who entertained her with local legends as he drove toward Lake Balaton.

Ava trailed behind the porter who carried her luggage on a huge cart down the long hallway covered with lush red carpet. She tipped him and threw herself on the bed, arms outstretched. "I can't believe I'm here!" she said, her head turned toward the large sliding glass doors that overlooked the calm water of the lake. She marveled at the classy pool that showcased the many tables and lounge chairs with oversized umbrellas.

She could just picture herself lying out there getting some well-needed sun. *But first, lunch,* she thought smiling when her stomach rumbled.

With a quick trip to the bathroom, she washed her face and applied some light makeup. She piled her long blonde hair into an updo and changed into a knee-length black cocktail dress. *This should be fine for a five-star eatery*, she thought as she glanced at her slim figure in the bathroom mirror.

After a delicious lunch of stuffed cabbage rolls and Gundel pancake for dessert, she returned to her room ready for a few hours of rest. Feeling exhausted, she slept through the afternoon and night, and the following morning she ordered room service and ate as she perused the booklet in her room that featured various places of interest to see in the area.

She dressed comfortably and decided to book the historical tour in the village of Tihany. The resort shuttle promptly left at 10 a.m. She had to quicken her step to catch it before it left without her. Taking a backseat on the shuttle allowed her to have some privacy and reflect on how blessed she felt at the moment to be able to take this trip.

She joined the group after departing the shuttle to listen to the guide who explained the schedule for the day and the time she'd need to be back at the bus. Glancing at her feet thought, *Glad I packed these old sneakers. They'll get some good use today.*

The tour of the huge Benedictine Abbey that was built in 1055 was the first stop, and its beauty was overwhelming, not to mention its size. Ava took several photos before they had moved deeper into the village where she was looking forward to shopping in the various pottery shops and having lunch in one of the quaint outdoor cafés.

The tour had exhausted her and even though it was almost dinnertime she took a well-needed nap on the comfy king-size bed.

Opening her eyes, she glanced over at the clock on the bedside table. "Six O'clock already? This clean air and walking all day are doing me good!"

She headed to the shower and then to the closet to select a dress that would be appropriate for the dining area. *Hmm, this red cocktail dress is just the ticket. Red has always seemed to give me more energy.*

A few stares were quite noticeable as she entered the stunning outdoor restaurant with a beautiful fountain in the center of the seating area. The hostess led her over to a table close to the fountain. Strings of small outdoor lights were strung along the walls making the alfresco area seem almost magical.

After ordering a glass of white wine she read the menu and couldn't help but notice a loud but friendly-looking young couple who had taken the table next to her. They had a pile of brochures and other literature that they had brought to their table along with a camera.

The young redhead turned to the hostess. "I'm sorry, ma'am. We don't mean to be so loud but we're nature photographers and so excited to be here. If we take a few shots of this gorgeous outdoor patio, please forgive us."

The hostess smiled and waved her hand to dismiss the woman's apology. "No problem at all. Enjoy your stay," she said.

The waitress took Ava's order and asked if anyone would be joining her. "No. I'll be dining alone," she stated with a sad smile.

The young redhead stared at her for a second with a sympathetic look and walked over to her table. "Sorry to bother you, I just heard you speak English. My name is Tessa Jergenson. My husband over there is Kevin. We are professional photographers and are here to take photos of the wildlife in the marsh, especially the birds. The Small Balaton is a huge wetland habitat that is unique in Europe. We're planning to go down to the river Zala delta tomorrow."

"Hello, I'm Ava. I hope you'll enjoy your adventure to the wetland. I prefer to relax and enjoy a quiet two weeks in the comfort of the hotel," she laughed.

Tessa took her hand. "We're so excited! The wetland has a large population of plant and animal species such as bee-eaters, cranes, and marvelous herons. The Small-Balaton area is also rich in other species of animals. European pond turtles, otters, ermine, martens, various species of dragonflies, and about 30 species of fish. Also, numerous species of orchids can be found there. Oh, sorry for bugging you, but I'm so excited about the trip and we can't find too many people who speak English."

"No bother at all!" Ava assured the chatty young woman. "Enjoy your adventure."

Tessa returned to her table and whispered to her husband that she felt a tone of loneliness in Ava's voice. "Maybe we should invite her to join us tomorrow," she suggested while picking up a menu.

Kevin nodded. "She didn't sound like she'd be into that sort of thing."

Ava couldn't help but overhear their muted conversation. *Hmm, so I see they feel sorry for me. I should put on a happy face, but no. I did that way too many times when I was married.*

After dinner Ava took a stroll around the grounds, admiring the lush vegetation and colored lights that lit up the pool area. A strong breeze had picked up and she rubbed her arms trying to erase the goosebumps. The all-so-familiar odd feeling came over her that always warned her of impending danger. *Perhaps it just signals a normal storm this time. I hope...* She headed back to her room to turn in for the night.

Right before she climbed under the covers, she looked at the other brochures, one featuring the Water Tower in the village's main square. She thought that if the storm was coming, she may not be able to do the tour. *Maybe that's what that feeling was I had out there and nothing more.* However, the uneasy feeling stayed with her and made her think of the countless disasters, accidents, and people getting hurt that followed after she experienced those eerie feelings.

She sighed and after looking through another brochure she became drowsy and quickly fell into a deep sleep.

The loud sound of the church bell had awakened Ava out of her deep slumber and the foul smell of rotten eggs filled her nose. She sat up in bed startled and nauseous. The clock showed 6 a.m. *Is there a fire? Perhaps here they sound the church bell instead of the fire alarm,* she thought as she rose quickly to look out of the large glass doors.

She saw a large plume of black smoke engulfing the back pool area. She quickly threw on her robe and made it to the lobby to see what had happened.

Several guests had congregated in the lobby as the desk clerk and manager had informed them all was okay now. There was a grease fire in the restaurant's kitchen. Firemen were called and were attending to the fire.

Ava shook with chills—the same ones she'd felt last night. *I just knew something bad was going to happen. I felt a storm may have been in the works but even so, my intuition is usually a natural alarm system.*

She had noticed Tessa and Kevin now rushing to the lobby and making their way over to her. "What's going on?" Tessa asked, her arms folded across her chest trying to ease the chill in the air.

"It was a grease fire in the kitchen, and it's being handled now. It's a peculiar custom in this area to use the church bell instead of the fire alarm," Ava replied.

"What?" Tessa asked looking confused. "The fire station must be close to the resort because the loud alarm scared me half to death. I didn't hear any church bells, did you hear it, Kevin?"

"Nope," Kevin scratched his chin. "But they have a helluva loud fire alarm system."

"Well, I guess we'll have to find a restaurant in town to get breakfast before we head south," Tessa said, scanning the lobby to see more firemen coming in and out of the building.

Hearing the conversation, the tall, lanky, desk clerk had come over with three food vouchers in his hand. They were for a local breakfast café within walking distance of the resort. "Compliments of the hotel," he said. "The restaurant should be cleaned up and back in business for the dinner hour."

"Well, I guess that solves that," Ava said, tying the belt on her robe a bit tighter.

"Let's have breakfast together. We'll meet you in the café," Tessa suggested.

Ava looked forward to having company during breakfast. She arrived at the small café early and was seated at an outdoor table as she waited for Tessa and Kevin. It was already 8:30 and her stomach was rumbling. The waiters were hoisting the umbrellas up on every table as the sun was already beating down.

She'd ordered a cappuccino while she waited for her company. Tessa and Kevin came strolling in fifteen minutes after appearing to be in quite a jovial mood. Both had huge smiles on their faces and hugs were exchanged.

"Let's eat and be on our way. We have an hour's drive ahead of us," Kevin said as he picked up a menu.

Tessa scooted her chair over to Ava. "Not sure if you have any plans today, but we wanted to invite you to accompany us on our birdwatching trip today. Don't know if you are into birds, but we are so excited to get some footage of the local wildlife there."

Ava took a sip of her latte. "How very sweet of you. I was going to venture over to the Water Tower, but I may take just take you up on that offer another day. I'm planning to rent a car tomorrow and drive around."

"We're going to find a hotel or a guesthouse in Zalaszabar, it's a small town located on the shore of the Small Balaton marshland. We can make a reservation for you as well, and you can come with us birdwatching if you change your mind."

Ava gave her a small smile and after exchanging phone numbers, the couple left in a hurry.

On the short walk back to the resort Ava became quite anxious thinking about going out in a small boat to the wetlands and felt a strange urge to go there. *Perhaps I'll join them. It's just a wetland and a few birds. How can this mean trouble?* she wondered. Just as she was nearing the lobby entrance, a dark, long-legged bird flew right above her head, almost knocking her out. "What the hell?" she shouted, noticing the large bird that now took off in a flash and with a few strands of her hair. She heard the church bell again, but she realized that she'd only heard the sound in her mind and not in her ears. *What does this mean? Just as I've been thinking about the wetland. Is it an omen to warn me not to go there? Or perhaps I must go there?*

***

Kevin and Tessa drove south enjoying the view. After renting a boat, they were excited to venture out onto the marshland. The weather was perfect—not a cloud in the sky. Kevin handed Tessa the waterproof case that contained all the equipment as he took a seat in the rear and grabbed a paddle. "I'm really hoping to catch sight of the grey herons!"

"We'll be lucky if we can find them," Tessa replied. "I'm excited to see dragonflies and rare orchids too," she said as she maneuvered the canoe to the right toward a narrow inlet that led into the wider area of the reeds.

About halfway down the inlet, Kevin mentioned to Tessa about the oddness there. The entire area was vacant of any wildlife. Even the reeds hung limp as though they were feeling tired. They spotted a few nests in the dry areas, but they appeared to be vacant.

"Maybe we made too much noise and need to move further on," Tessa suggested.

"Not sure what's going on, but this is most unusual," Kevin said as he reached for the camera pack. "I'll just try to get a few shots of this deserted area though. It does hold a unique beauty."

Just as Kevin reached for the waterproof case, the boat shook and hit bottom. They were in an area thick with dead reeds. The more they tried to get the boat to move the more it became idle as if they were stuck to the very spot.

"Guess, we'll need to find a footpath, get out of here and walk back!" Tessa shouted. "I mean, the rental place has to understand why we just left the boat here."

Kevin refused to give up. "I'll get in the water, and you steer the boat as hard as you can," he said.

With Tessa helping to guide the boat and Kevin's pushing, the boat finally gave way and was cut loose from the spot.

"I tell you, that was odd," Kevin said, breathless.

12

"To say the least," Tessa admitted. "It's a good thing Ava didn't come. I don't think she would have enjoyed standing in murky water."

As they maneuvered the boat from the thick reeds to the open water, they were stunned to see the rolling dark clouds that were hidden from them by the thick wall of reeds and heard the deep rumble of the impending storm. "Let's get out of here!" Kevin shouted, paddling faster.

***

Ava was enjoying the tour of the Water Tower and listening to the guide tell the history of it being the main source of drinking water and fire water in the town until World War II when it was used as an observation station by the Germans. Now fully renovated the tower was used as a tourist attraction with an elevator and boasted the best lookout. She decided she'd have lunch in the café then take the resort shuttle back and have a short nap.

Shortly before she had drifted off, she thought about the Jergensons and wondered if they had gotten any worthy pictures of the wildlife.

Ava had gotten a call from the main desk that the resort restaurant was up and running that evening, and she was surprised to get a call from her new friends that they'd been back, reserved a table, and hoped she would join them.

No sooner had she passed by the main desk when she saw Tessa waving to her from across the room.

"I'm so glad you could join us tonight," Tessa said, hugging Ava.

"What happened? I thought you were staying at the guest house down south. How was your trip to the marshland?"

"Well, we did run into some issues, and odd ones at that. We got nothing today. I mean, it was like a 'dead zone' out there. Then to top it off, our boat ran aground, and even though the weather report promised a sunny day, an unexpected storm erupted. So, we decided to drive back and stay here until the storm passes."

Ava froze upon hearing those words. Another odd feeling came over her. She smelled the foul stench of sulfur and in her mind's eye saw a large body of murky water and heard the church bell again.

"Ava… you okay?" Tessa asked, taking ahold of Ava's arm.

"Oh, yes, just... It must be a gas leak in the kitchen, for a second, I smelled rotten eggs..."

"I don't smell anything," Tessa sniffed the air and shook her head.

"I don't smell it anymore," Ava gave her a nervous smile. "It must have been the breeze…"

"Well, we do plan to go out again as soon as the weather clears up. We do need to have something to show our boss upon our return."

Kevin joined them. Tessa had informed her husband that she had already filled Ava in on the details of the day's strange outing. While enjoying their cocktails the waiter arrived and went over the dinner specials. All three of them decided to go with the onion soup and fried carp. Kevin kept repeating how strange the trip to the wetland was as Ava tried to connect those events to the feelings she had about the bird attacking her. She didn't mention any of this to them for fear they'd think she was crazy. She quickly changed the subject by sharing her pictures of the Water Tower.

During dessert, Ava couldn't help but notice a tall dark-haired man taking a seat at the table next to them. He was well-dressed in a most expensive-looking suit. And Tessa couldn't help but notice Ava's long stare.

"He is quite handsome," Tessa whispered into Ava's ear. "And if I'm not mistaken, he just smiled at you."

Ava's face turned bright red, and she turned back around to finish her dessert.

Kevin and Tessa decided to retire early and just as Ava had picked up her evening bag and stood up, the tall handsome stranger approached her. "Sorry, but I couldn't help hearing your conversation. I hear your friends are here to take photos of wildlife. I'm an

Ornithologist, and I'm here to study birds in the same area. Oh, please forgive me, my name is Maxwell Baker. They call me Max."

"Please to meet you, Max," Ava offered her hand gazing into his deep chocolate eyes.

"I see you are about to leave but would you like to sit with me and have a drink while I dine? I hate to eat alone," Max asked, releasing Ava's hand.

"I'd… I'd love to," she hesitated a little.

Max had ordered another cocktail for Ava and a light dinner for himself. After finishing his meal, he proceeded to talk about his profession and position at the university as a professor in London. Ava sat mesmerized listening to all the details about his work with so many species of birds from all over the world.

It was clear there was some real chemistry going on between the two of them. Ava's heart leaped when Max invited her to join him in his birdwatching. She wasn't quick to reply, with Max taking notice. "I guess you have plans, or maybe don't fancy nature outings?" he asked.

"No—it's just—well, maybe another time." She looked away at the fountain that seemingly sounded louder than she'd remembered.

"Look, I promise it's all safe, and since I'm a pro, you have nothing to worry about," Max rattled off hoping to convince Ava.

She sighed and before she could think it over, she replied with a yes. *Why did I agree?* She thought feeling panic settling into her core. "But the Jegensons said there is a nasty storm down there," she said, trying to take back her promise.

"Oh, it will be over tonight. It's going to be a beautiful, sunny day tomorrow."

"Okay," she hesitated and sighed. "What time do you want to leave?"

"How about 9 a.m. sharp? I've rented a car, so we don't have to be on a schedule as the shuttle is."

"I'll be ready."

What the hell was I thinking? she thought as she made her way back to her room. *I don't want this trip to end up the way it did with the Jergensons. And I didn't get any weird feelings when he touched my hand. Instead, his touch gave me a sense of comfort.*

Ava tossed and turned most of the night, thinking about her trip with Max. She'd managed to get a few hours of restless sleep but woke to the blaring alarm on her phone at 7:30 a.m.

Rushing to get dressed, she texted the Jergensons to apologize for not going with them and to let them know of her plans with Max. She wished them a better day if they were attempting to get back to their birdwatching adventure. Tessa texted back letting her know that they were on their way already. *We might even see you there.* She finished her text.

Max was waiting down in the lobby for Ava while she was running a few minutes late. She wanted to pull up some information on the area, but the Wi-Fi was not working.

"You are a vision," Max said as Ava approached in her khaki shorts and fitted white T-shirt.

She blushed, thanked him, and pulled her straw hat out of the small backpack she brought.

"That's quite some backpack you have there," she replied, noticing it was one of those expensive backpacks she'd seen on survivalist shows.

He opened the passenger side door for her then proceeded to open the trunk and set both of their backpacks in. "I have a good feeling about this trip," he said. "I feel like we'll find something very valuable besides birds."

During the drive, Ava told him about the strange feelings she'd had before the kitchen fire and her friend's outing. Realizing how freely she talked about things she hesitated to open up to Tessa and Kevin, Ava felt stunned. *He's a total stranger and yet I feel I've known him for all my life and for some strange reason, I trust him.*

Max listened and not even a hint of mocking in his voice asked, "You must be a Sensitive. As I said, I often have feelings about upcoming events too."

Ava sighed. "Not sure, but I do know this type of thing has been happening to me since my teens."

"Well, it may come in handy during our expedition," Max replied. "Usually, intuitive people can also pick up feelings from wildlife as well."

Ava smiled and then turned to gaze out the window, admiring all the huge poplar trees that lined the road. "You were right," she laughed. "The weather is beautiful today."

Max took care of the boat rental details as she made a quick inspection of the items in the backpack. She reached for her sunscreen and applied it lavishly to her fair skin. She thought about Max's olive skin tone and wondered if he used sunscreen or if it was simply his natural Greek heritage to have such a lovely tone.

After setting his equipment up in the boat, he helped Ava in and handed her a life vest. "Oh, I'm a great swimmer," she said.

"It's the policy with the rental company," he said.

Ava tied on the vest as Max did his and they paddled off toward the larger area of the wetland that he'd indicated he wanted to go. He'd told her it was where the bigger birds were.

As they approached the wider expanse of the reeds, he maneuvered the boat closer to the bank where he noticed many empty nests. "Let's get out here so I can take some samples from the nests," he said, reaching for his small specimen cases in his bag.

Ava stood by his side on the banks as she watched him gently tear off some pieces of the nest and place them in the case. "This is quite odd. I've never seen so many nests with eggs in them and no sign of birds."

His statement gave Ava goosebumps as she suddenly felt the air around her turning chilly. She rubbed her arms trying to warm up.

Max noticed her unsettled behavior and told her he had gotten what he needed, and they'd be on their way back. Ava kept her eyes on the sky noticing the grey clouds that had moved in along with a sudden breeze.

They were not too far off from the dock when a flock of herons flew right above the boat almost grazing the top of Max's head.

"Jeez! That was weird!" he yelled, halting his paddling.

Ava didn't have much to offer other than a 'yes'.

Max was quite talkative on the short drive back to the resort, but Ava was quiet, trying to process all the strangeness that had occurred.

When Max asked her if she'd join him the following day on another trip to the wetland, she was quick to reply with an excuse. She told him she was going to spend the afternoon doing more sightseeing or laying out by the pool.

Being observant, Max knew she wasn't about to risk another quirky trip but invited her to dine with him, and she was quick to accept that offer. She felt that was a much safer choice.

Max walked Ava back to her room as the two stood in the doorway, both in an awkward mood, due to the nature of the day's events. Max was the first to break the ice. "Look, I know today wasn't so great, but I will make it up to you." He took hold of her hand. "I know you've had some pretty weird experiences since you got here."

Ava held his gaze. "Yes, to say the least."

Max had offered to take her out to one of the recommended restaurants in the village and she gladly accepted.

After enjoying a lovely dinner Max suggested a stroll on the beach or in town. Ava readily agreed. They strolled along the quaint shops eyeing so many exquisite handmade items from the locals. When they approached a metaphysical shop Ava felt a strong pull to go inside and check it out. Maybe it was the fact that the shop was mostly dark but illuminated with a variety of colored candles. When they entered the shop a tingling of bells had alerted the store clerk that there were customers.

A petite middle-aged lady emerged from the back room wearing a long purple caftan. "May I help you?" she asked, adjusting her glasses that had sat on the bridge of her nose.

"No, we are just browsing," Max said, not making eye contact with her.

Ava trailed behind Max as they perused the interesting items in the shop. On a display in the back, a bronze statue of a bird had caught Max's eye. The clerk was on his tail ready to make a sale. "This bird dates back to the fifteenth century. It's a falcon and was repurchased from an older woman here in the village who is known to be psychic among the locals.

Ava's ears perked up with the mention of 'psychic'. *Hmm, maybe I should go and see this lady? She may have an answer as to why I'm having so many odd premonitions.*

Ava's ears had perked up when the clerk had mentioned that this psychic knew many old legends, especially the one about the famous 'Cursed Church Bell'.

Max took out his valet. "I'll buy the statue and I'd also like to know the name of this psychic you spoke of."

The clerk was more than happy to provide the name as she wrote it on a small card and placed it in the bag with the statue that she'd wrapped in tissue paper.

After departing the shop Max suggested they stop for a drink at a small outdoor café two doors down. He was anxious to take a look at the name on the card.

He pulled out his reading glasses from his pocket making sure he read the name right. Galeena Danos was written on a small business card from the shop. There was no phone number nor an address. "Now how in the world am I supposed to find this woman?" he asked, turning to Ava.

"This is a small town. I'm sure if you ask someone here in the café they could tell you," She suggested.

Max and Ava enjoyed their cocktails before Max had taken up Ava's suggestion. He asked the young waiter who had told him that he would ask his boss for information.

Ten minutes had gone by when an older balding man in a checkered apron approached their table and took a seat. He reached his hand out for a handshake. "I'm Dominic Horvath, the owner. I hear you are looking for Galeena Danos."

"Yes, we are," replied Max, keeping eye contact with the man, "do you know where I can find her?"

"I do but first I need to know of your intentions. In this town, we all protect one another. A few years ago, we had some reporters come who did not have the best of intentions and since then we have been most protective of our village and its people. I hope you can understand this."

Max and Ava both said 'yes' in unison and shared their stories about the oddness of the marsh and Ava's premonitions.

The owner nodded, pulled out a small piece of paper from his apron, and jotted down Galeena's address, but no phone, which Max was quick to question.

"It's no use in me providing you with this, as she does not have a mobile and only a landline and most likely would hang up on you. So, I suggest you go to visit her. It's not far from here, but don't go in the dark."

Max took the paper and thanked Mr. Horvath. He tucked it in his pocket along with the other card.

Ava looked up at Max, "Well, how soon are you going to see her?"

"You mean how soon are *we* going to see her?" he replied, taking her hand. "I guess tomorrow morning."

"Perfect," she said. "I'm curious myself to hear this legend."

Ava enjoyed a quick breakfast with the Jergensons in the outdoor café. They had claimed to have gone to the wetland with no luck, just as she and Max experienced.

Max was prompt and both headed to the village with much anticipation to talk to Galeena.

The GPS had led them on the small brick road to the far end of the village. Ava gasped as they pulled up to the modest stone cottage. "To tell you the truth, I'm kinda scared to knock on the door. What if she's a dark witch or worse?"

"What could be worse?" Max chuckled.

"It's not funny. Ever since I arrived here, it's been one strange thing after the next!"

Max was over-eager to hear some good urban tales. He knocked on the solid oak door twice. Ava hid behind him. The door slowly creaked open as an elderly lady in a paisley babushka peeked her head through. "Can I help you?" she asked, speaking Hungarian.

To her surprise, Max spoke fluid Hungarian and introduced himself and Ava then explained the nature of their visit and reassured the old woman that they were not reporters. He promised not to keep her long.

Galeena ushered them in and led them into her small living area which consisted of an overstuffed sofa, a recliner, and two oak tables. There was an old stone fireplace in the corner.

Max and Ava sat on the sofa across from Galeena who sat in the chair. Max and Ava, both informed her of everything that they had encountered. And they watched the old woman whose face was etched with numerous wrinkles listening intently.

Galeena was not one to be shy as she quickly asked. "So, I understand you are here to learn some of the history of our village. I could go on for days as we do, indeed have a rich history but let me begin with what I think you came to hear."

Ava scooted to the edge of the sofa to make eye contact with Galeena. "I first want to thank you for taking the time to do this."

"My pleasure, dear, and let me say that I am picking up some vibes from you that tell me you are quite possibly a strong Sensitive."

"Well, it's got to be something, because it's been happening since I was a child."

Galeena went on to tell her story of the cursed church bell, which was a gift from the most talented craftsman in all of Hungary. The bell had been given to him for repair decades ago by a church from the east side of Hungary, but they never claimed it. However, after the bell was installed, strange things started happening whenever they sounded the bell.

Max and Ava listened with intent, not interrupting as Galeena went on. "When the bell would ring in the church, people would become nervous and afraid, and most of them would avoid attending mass. Even the birds flew off and small animals scurried away. Neighbors fought with each other, and people became anxious every time that bell rang. The church leaders knew something was amiss and all decided to bury the bell as it may have been cursed, so they buried it back on the church property."

"So, did this solve the problem?" Max asked.

"It did not. It seemed the only way to block the curse was to bury it deep underwater. They were advised to do this only after seeking help from the village wise man."

"So, I assume it's still here?" Max asked, leaning forward on the sofa.

"As far as I know."

"Well, that may explain the odd effect it may still have on the birds in the wetland," Max surmised.

"That it may," she said while tucking some strands of gray hair back in her babushka. "Can I offer you both some tea?"

Max and Ava both declined and thanked Galeena for her time.

Galeena took ahold of Ava's hand as they reached the door. "You have a gift my dear but use it wisely. The more you learn to trust your intuition, the stronger it will work for you."

Ava thanked her and noticed how her blue eyes sparkled as she spoke. She intuitively knew this woman also had a gift.

On the ride back to the resort Max was full of excitement telling Ava he planned on going back to the wetland the following day to do more investigating.

Ava shook her head, "You do have a curious nature, but I'll pass on another trip but would love to meet you tomorrow evening for dinner."

"I'm looking forward to it," Max replied with a smile.

That evening they enjoyed a relaxing dinner in a small but elegant restaurant in the village. The locals had recommended it as it was touted to have some of the best Hungarian food in the area.

Max had complimented Ava on her stunning black cocktail dress trimmed with sequins. "You don't need sequins to shine, my dear."

Ava blushed and steered the conversation toward Max's journey back to the wetland. "I want you to know I have a bad feeling about this."

Max was positive, as it was his nature. "I'm sure I will be okay. Whatever this thing is, legend or not, it intrigues me."

After the hour-long drive back to Siofok, Max had invited Ava over to his suite for a drink, but she felt a strange urge to go back to her room. As she walked through the open walkways, she felt anxious.

She calmed down in her room and fell asleep fast. Just as the sun was coming up, she woke to a small tremor that shook the room. She heard the church bell in her mind, again. "What in the world!" She sat up in bed but was too scared to move. The hotel's intercom came to life. The desk clerk had informed the guests that there had been a small earthquake not far from the resort and all was well.

Her mobile was ringing, and it was Max. He was calling to make sure she was okay. He reassured her that this is common in the area and not to be rattled. Hearing his voice had helped somewhat but she did inform him of the weird feelings she had had the previous night. "You know, Galeena is right. I probably am a Sensitive and always have been."

Max agreed and she asked him if he was still planning on making another trip to the wetland.

"Nothing's gonna stop me, not even a little shaking."

Ava shook her head, intuitively expecting that response. "Well, I'm going to check on the Jergensons and I will see you later tonight after you get back."

Tessa answered the phone quite startled due to the quake and had informed her that she and Kevin were planning to leave and return to Boston. Their boss had plans to send them on another assignment. Tessa also had confided in her that she felt there was something truly odd about the whole place. Ava didn't add in her two cents, not wanting to fuel the fire but wished them well and promised to keep in touch before she ended the call. She sat on the edge of the bed glancing at the clock on the side table. Her stomach was rumbling from hunger, and she needed her coffee, earthquake or not.

She quickly dressed and headed to the resort café for breakfast. She'd gotten a text from Max that he was already packing the car. Having the day to herself she decided to make a reservation at the spa. A well-needed massage may just be what she needed.

***

Max was pleased to hear the boat rental agency was up and running after the earthquake. He was eager to get back out into the wetland. He wished Ava had accompanied him, but he knew she had her reservations. After loading all of his gear into the rowboat he paddled toward the same inlet that led into the larger reserve. It was a cloudy day but not too cool. "He looked up to see a large heron flying above. "That's just what I came for!"

Ahead he noticed a few cranes nestled among the reeds, so he moored the boat toward the bank slowly, trying not to scare them off. He dismounted the boat as his thick rubber boots sunk into the thick, wet reeds. He had the camera ready and was adjusting his settings to get the perfect shot. As soon as the camera had made two clicks the herons took off.

There's got to be more birds further down, he thought as he put his equipment back in the boat. Rowing further down the wetland he saw something metallic sticking out of the muddy water. He maneuvered the boat over to get a better look. "What the heck?"

As he approached closer, he could tell it looked like a large bell. He put on his gloves and tried to pull it up. *Hmm, this must have been unearthed due to the quake.* He examined the bell closely. It took both hands to lift it halfway out of the mud. "I wonder if this is the bell Galeena spoke of? I've got to get it into the boat and take it to shore."

After some hard pull, shove, and push, he managed to drag the heavy bell into the boat. He pulled his muddy gloves off and grabbed the bell to steady it in the middle of the boat when suddenly, a deep dread washed over him. He broke out in a cold sweat and never felt so anxious before. *I've got to get out of here!* He panicked and leaving everything behind, he jumped out of the boat, dragging his feet in the knee-deep mud, hurrying toward the drier-looking footpath.

It took Max about half an hour to reach the shore. The owner of the boat rental looked at him with wide eyes while he told him where he left the boat. "The cursed church bell…" the man whispered. "It is true. I'm going to call the museum; they'll know what to do with it."

After the helpers at the rental place towed the boat to the dock, Max took his backpack, kicked off his muddy boots, and got into his car. As soon as he drove away, the panicky feeling was gone.

∗∗∗

After an hour of pleasant driving, Max found Ava in the hotel's restaurant having lunch with Tessa and Kevin. "You won't believe what happened!" he said, catching his breath as he sat down. "The legend the psychic told us about is true! I felt it."

A few days later Max and Ava visited the museum and found out that they had cleaned and tested the old bell. They assumed that possibly the bellmaker, not knowing that the metal he used to repair the bell would change the frequency of the sound. The low frequency of the repaired bell had set off vibrations that triggered anxiety and panic in Sensitive people. They decided to display the bell in a soundproof case to prevent even accidentally sounding the bell by anyone.

The vacation time came to an end, but the chemistry between Ava and Max grew even stronger. A year later, Tessa and Kevin got an invitation to their wedding that would be held in the Azur Hotel in Siofok.

The Zanna

By David W. Thompson

Dear Diary,

I know it has been a while since I've written to you...not since Mommy's accident two years ago. I forgot to take you home with me last summer, diary, but I guess I haven't had much to say...or write since then anyway. I just didn't want to talk about any of it anymore. Daddy said it must've been an accident when Mommy slipped, but there are constant reminders. Grown-ups are always asking about everything. I don't know what I would do if it wasn't for my best friend Zanna.

"How are you coping, Elena?" They always asked. "Do you miss your mommy?" (Duh!).

"Are you doing OK, sweetheart?" Well, no I'm not. OK? I am not happy! I don't know if I'll ever be happy again!

Then it would be "How's your father doing? And little Sam?" Daddy is sad, he's always sad now. Sam doesn't remember much. So, please stop asking. Just leave us in peace. OK? Peace and quiet, that's all we need.

I don't know why Daddy wanted to come here...again this summer. He knows how much I've hated camping ever since Mommy's accident. He said this was his memorial to Mommy, to come here every year like we did in the past before... everything. I think Mommy would rather be left in peace to sleep. Thank goodness Daddy let me bring Zanna with us again this year. He'd promised to take Sam and me to the beach, but the new woman Jessica, she hates the beach you know. No surprise then, here we are at this old cabin.

When we came last year, I got covered with a rash all over me. Poison Ivy Daddy said and it itched like crazy too. I think I caught it by the old abandoned well behind the outhouse. We always throw our table scraps in there. Only Daddy and me know about the old well. Oh and Zanna. She knows too, of course. We're all good at keeping secrets.

Oh, and another thing about camping. I hate biting bugs! And my sleeping bag smells old and moldy, like our basement at home. Daddy won't let me play there but I wouldn't want to anyway. It's dark and scary. One time I thought I heard Mommy crying in the dark down there. Daddy said it was just my imagination, but Zanna heard it too. I bet Jessica wishes I lived down there. She tells Daddy that children should be seen, not heard, but I think she'd rather I wasn't seen either...

Anyway, I'm lying on my stinky old sleeping bag while I write this. Zanna and I spread the bag out to share as a pad under us and we'll pull a blanket over us to sleep tonight. I don't want to sleep on that stained mattress in the room we share with Sam. It looks like a prop from those murder mystery shows that Daddy says I can't watch. He says I'm young and impressionable. That's his nice way of saying I'm immature and corruptible. The stains look like dried blood or something worse and I think a mouse is living in it too. I can hear it scratching in there now.

Well, I'm getting tired, dear diary, it was a long drive getting here, but I'll write more later. Maybe my writing to you will keep Zanna and me from being bored or going mad. Elena Darie, 12 years old last week. Happy birthday to me.

Dear Diary,

Things have gotten worse since Elena wrote to you last. She said we could share you and we both promised not to read what the other wrote.

It's only our third night here and already Elena's legs are covered with bites. It looks like she has some kind of skin disease...like leprosy maybe? Her daddy says it's the "skeeters" getting her but I saw a spider on the window in our room too. We're not scared of spiders but I wish they wouldn't bite us or crawl on us while we're sleeping. The bugs don't bother Sam, even though we sleep in the same room. Jessica told Elena it was because she's so fat and eats too much candy. She says that's why bugs like her sweet blood. Mr. Darie cut his eyes at her when she said that but he didn't say anything.

I whispered in Elena's ear when I saw her eyes misting up. "Don't let her see you cry. You can't let people see that you're weak or that they're getting to you." I knew her mommy always told her that. Still, it didn't help her mommy any.

Spiders and skeeters aren't the only critters around here. Sam caught a snake today and Jessica screamed when he showed it to her. It was just a little old green snake. I wish he'd thrown it at her, but Sam isn't like that. He doesn't like her either though. Jessica told Elena that she was her daddy's new girlfriend and she might as well get used to the idea. Elena told me she wished her daddy would send Jessica away. But what if Jessica was making him happy? He's been so sad...what if he sent her away instead? I don't know what Elena would do then... I'm worried about her.

Talk soon. Love, Zanna

Dear Diary,

Guess what? Our cabin's roof leaks. I dreamt Sam was squirting me with his water-blaster pistol & I woke up with wet hair and a soaked sleeping bag. I went out on the cabin's covered porch to watch the storm. It felt funny out there. Not "ha-ha" funny, you know. but "weird" funny. I think someone was secretly watching the cabin, but I couldn't tell for sure. The cold rain brought with it a low-hanging fog that encircled the outhouse and the secret well. It smothered everything in its ghostly arms. While I stared, the bushes started shaking. Was something...or someone in there? I think there was. I think it was Mommy. She never slept well at night, but she was awake now...and she was hungry. I told Daddy she wouldn't want us coming back here.

Your friend always, Elena

P.S. Zanna and me didn't tell Sam about what we thought. He gets scared so easily.

Dear Diary,

When Jessica came to breakfast this morning, she acted happy for a change. Daddy teased her saying she was flitting around the room like a butterfly on the verbena bush in our backyard. I thought she looked like a cockroach on a puddle of syrup and smiled to myself. I shoved a forkful of the toaster waffles that Daddy made in my mouth to keep from laughing out loud. Jessica didn't like us laughing at the dining table. Odd too, because she was such a loud person most of the time. I love the quiet. It was the one part of camping I enjoyed, but there was no peace and quiet when Jessica was with us.

"What do you find so hysterically humorous, child?" she screeched in my ear. "I know that eating is your favorite pastime, but try to restrain yourself. Look at your brother and try to behave like he does."

I glanced over at Sam. He was staring at his plate. His food was untouched and his lips were drawn into a tight straight line.

"May I please be excused, Miss Jessica?" he asked.

"Of course you may, Sam, but first, can I ask you something?"

Sam nodded his head and looked at me.

"How would you like to have a new mommy, Sam?" Jessica asked.

Sam pushed back from the table, but not before I saw the tears welling up in his eyes.

"I'm...I'm ...I'm not..." Sam always stutters when he is upset.

"You'll never be our mommy, Jessica," I said.

She smiled then, a wide smile that did not reach her eyes, or perhaps painted them even darker. My friend Zanna calls it her snarky smile, a humorless smile projecting an evil resolve.

"Oh no. Not your mother, I'm sure. Your mother is dead...dead...dead. How do you like the new necklace your daddy gave me?" she asked and shook it at me. I said it looked just like Mommy's old one. Daddy made a face and shook his head. I got up and retrieved a picture of our family from the living room. It was the one with Mommy wearing a necklace that looked just like Jessica's. Everyone looked so happy in the picture. I held it up for Jessica to see. She grabbed the picture out of my hand and threw it across the room. I heard the glass break away from the frame. I hated her more than ever just then...

"It's time you adjusted to your new situation, young lady. I won't put up with your disrespect." Jessica's face was the color of a boiled lobster.

"Daddy, I think the necklace looked better on Mommy, don't you?" I asked.

Jessica slapped me and it split my lip. I tasted blood and sucked it in so she wouldn't see. Daddy jumped up and his chair hit the floor but I'm not sure what he said. The room was spinning. I retrieved the family picture and flipped back my hair (something Jessica hates). I stalked off to my room with my head held high. I managed to close the door behind me before the sobbing started. Zanna came with me and hugged me tight, but I couldn't stop crying until my throat started hurting. I was glad that Sam didn't see. He would tell Daddy.

Love, Elena

Dear Diary,

I know Elena already wrote you early this morning, but everyone is in bed now and there's more to tell you. Mr. Darie and Jessica got into a big fight tonight. It was worse than the fight he had with Elena's mommy two years ago. Sam woke us up because he had to pee and didn't want to go out to the outhouse in the dark by himself. Elena and I went out with him, and we heard strange scratching noises. It was under the outhouse and sounded like rats in a wall trying to claw their way out...or in. Sam was afraid but Elena hugged him and told him not to worry. He's a sweet little boy but he scares so easily. I told him it was just his mommy waking up and that settled him down.

When we got back to our room, Sam asked if he could sleep on the floor with us and we told him he could. He was asleep in minutes. I don't know how he slept through everything that happened next though, but he did mumble in his sleep some and even cried out once...

Yours truly,

Zanna

Dear Diary,

I see that Zanna wrote to you last night so I may be repeating some things (I didn't read what she wrote, I promise). But I wanted to write down my thoughts anyway. Sam fell asleep within minutes of returning from our visit to the outhouse. Not long after, things got loud in the other bedroom, Zanna tapped me on the shoulder and we slipped out of our room to listen at their door.

"What did you expect me to do? Let that little brat mock me and sneer in my face?" Jessica asked.

"All of the experts say when a stepparent enters the picture, it's best to present a united front, especially in regards to discipline. That said, if you ever touch my children again, we are done. Do you understand me?"

"I will ruin you, Samuel. I think you forget yourself. I'm the only thing between you and bankruptcy. Your precious children will be motherless and homeless without me. Have you forgotten that as well? My signed check is waiting on the dresser in our bedroom at home for your deposit. It would be even easier to rip it into a million pieces than it was to write it. Now, do we have an understanding?"

"You can only push me so far, Jessica, and that line is my children. You need an old local family name to cement your political ambitions...and you want mine. You need me as much as I do you."

"If that prepubescent brat is the line you're drawing in the sand, Samuel, you damn well better keep her on the other side of that line. Life would be so much easier if she was away somewhere in a boarding school, and the further away the better. There's a good one in Morton County. They'd teach her some manners and beat a dose of respect into her."

I'd heard enough by then. I felt like I was the cause of all of Daddy's problems. I was the reason he wasn't happy anymore, why he never smiled. As quietly as I could, I slipped back to our room and under our blanket. I didn't close the door because of the creaking noise it makes like the doors do in movies about haunted houses. After a few minutes though, Zanna put her finger to her lips for me to be quiet. I heard the bedroom door creak open and I pretended to be sleeping. I wasn't sure what Jessica might do if she knew we'd been listening.

I prayed to Mommy for hours after that until I fell asleep. Zanna said Mommy would know what to do.

Breakfast awaits. Love, Elena

Dear Diary,

At breakfast, I put the family picture between Sam's plate and mine so we could look at it while we were eating.

"Your mother was a very sentimental person too, Elena," Daddy smiled. I added that she hated camping too.

"I'll tell you what I hate," Jessica said. She stood up from the table and pulled a trash bag out from the cabinet under the sink. "I hate all these ancient gloomy pictures everywhere and this family's morbid nostalgia. The woman is dead." She grabbed the picture from beside my plate before I could snatch it back. Then she stomped around the house removing all the pictures that had Mommy in them from the walls and tables. She tossed them all in the trash bag, frames and all. I could hear the glass break. Sam sat with his eyes and mouth opened wide. Daddy didn't say anything but wiped his eyes and cleared his throat. Zanna whispered in my ear and I repeated her thoughts out loud.

"I wish Jessica could meet Mommy," I said.

"Do you mean like Abby did? No, Elena." Daddy frowned.

Jessica swooped back into the room like the black clouds of a gathering thunderstorm. Her eyes flashed and the expression on her face meant it was about to get nasty. Her voice was like thunder when the lightning struck too close.

"And who might this Abby be?" she screeched.

"Abby wasn't anyone you'd know, Jessica," Daddy said. "She was a woman I dated last year."

"Last year? Exactly when was this?"

"Abby and I went out for a while, Jessica, but It was months before you and I met each other. And it didn't last long," Daddy said.

"How long?"

"Until Abby met Mommy," I said under my breath. Zanna giggled.

"Do you have something you want to say, Miss Smart Mouth Elena?"

"Nothing, Miss Jessica. May we be excused, Daddy?"

"We?" Jessica snarled. "You and Zanna both, you mean?"

"Yes you may," Daddy said and winked at me.

I didn't go to my room though, or at least, not right away. I went to the refrigerator and took out the old coffee can we used to store scraps and spoiled leftovers.

"I'll toss this stuff out. I'm sure there's something hungry outside that will enjoy it," I said.

"Not too close to the cabin, Elena. We don't need any rats," Jessica said.

"You know where to dump it, right, Elena?" Daddy asked.

I nodded my head but Daddy shook his. "Be careful."

Even with the bright morning light, it was dark inside the well. It reminded me of a cavern tour we did years ago when I was little. Sam wasn't born yet and I hadn't met Zanna, so it was just Mommy, Daddy, and me. Our tour guide told us if we'd stand very still, she'd cut off the already subdued lights. When she did, a shiver ran down my back. Mommy touched my hand and I almost jumped out of my skin. The well reminded me of that cave. I pulled the dead evergreen away from the opening and dumped the contents of the can inside. I heard the leftovers hit wet mud at the bottom. Then something moved!

Slap. Slap. Slap. Slap! Something was running on all fours across the wet bottom!

My hands were shaking as I pulled the brush back over the opening.

"Mommy?" I yelled, but there was no answer.

Something whined. It sounded like a hungry puppy. I ran back to the house so fast that Zanna could barely keep up. I curled up under the covers of my sleeping bag. Zanna said I was being so silly. Mommy would never hurt me.

That's all for now, Elena

Dear Diary,

This has to be a secret for now. Last night while Elena and Sam were asleep, Mr. Darie and that hateful Jessica got into it again. I snuck out of our bedroom and listened at the door. I'd do anything to protect my friend. Eavesdropping was the least thing. I'd overcome worse moral dilemmas since we'd met.

The argument was their usual, of course. Jessica was determined to send my friend away to some boarding school. It concerned me that Mr. Darie was less adamant than usual advocating for his daughter. Instead of putting Jessica in her place, he told her that she'd never given Elena a chance. That she should try and be friends with her and be nice to her for a change. If that didn't work, they would reassess the situation if she convinced him she'd put in the effort!

Jessica was down on Elena from day one. He was right about that much. I'm angry and I'm hurt. But what can I do to help my friend? We will see what tomorrow brings.

Yours truly, Zanna

Dear Diary,

Daddy was bugging me after lunch today. He wanted me and Jessica to try to be friends. So, I took Jessica for a walk. She promised to be nice and said we could get to know each other better. Daddy thought it was a good idea too. I didn't want to go but I'd do it for Daddy. As we were putting on our hiking boots, Zanna whispered in my ear.

"Zanna wants to know if she can come too?" I asked.

"Can't Zanna speak for herself?"

I looked at Zanna and shrugged my shoulders. Jessica said, "Sure, why not? The more the merrier. Anything to get away from this mausoleum your father calls a vacation cabin."

Jessica and I talked as we walked, but Zanna didn't say anything, only listened. I don't think she was happy with me or with Jessica either—especially when Jessica started asking me questions about her.

"So when did you first meet Zanna? Have the two of you been friends for very long?" she asked.

"For a few years. I was camping with my Girl Scout troop and Zanna came into my tent by mistake. She was so silly really."

"Your father said she told you she was a "Zanna"? And they were like fairies or something that protect little children from harm?"

I looked at Zanna and smiled. "Yes, something like that. I told you she was silly at first. Zanna is my age. How could she protect anyone? But we got talking and she told me her mommy was sometimes mean to her daddy. Her mommy was going to take her away from her daddy and she said mine would too if I wasn't careful."

"Why can't I see Zanna?"

Zanna yelled in my ear. "Because I don't want her to!"

I asked Zanna not to yell and told Jessica what she'd said.

"I used to have an imaginary friend when I was your age too, Elena," Jessica said. "I guess we do have something in common."

Zanna screamed in my ear. "Liar! Liar! She's a liar!"

"Stop, Zanna," I yelled. She didn't like Jessica either and sometimes she got jealous.

Zanna whispered in my ear again.

"Zanna wants me to show you something on the way back to the cabin," I told Jessica. "She says she'll let you see her then."

"That would be great, I'm looking forward to meeting her," she said.

"She's a liar," Zana said. "She'll take your daddy away, or she will send you away, Elena."

I didn't believe her, diary. If you remember, Daddy said we'd always be together after Mommy died.

"She's a liar!" Zanna screamed. "Liar, liar- pants on fire!"

"Did you say something?" Jessica asked.

"No, I was listening to Zanna."

I took the shortcut through the woods back towards the cabin. For a while, both Jessica and Zanna were quiet and I could tell Jessica was getting nervous.

"Where are you taking me, Elena? Are we lost?"

"Look over there," I said. "That's what we wanted you to see."

I took Jessica's hand and led her to a stump at the edge of the secret well.

"You don't want me to sit on that dirty old stump do you?"

There was some moss growing on top and I brushed it off as best I could.

"No, that won't do, Elena. I have good pants on."

I slipped off my jacket and laid it over the stump. It was getting warm outside anyway.

"I'm not going to scrub the stains out of that new jacket, Elena. Your father just bought that for you. Do you think money grows on trees?"

"You promised you'd be nice, Jessica."

"So I did." Her face scrunched up, but she sat down. "And you promised I'd get to meet your imaginary friend Zanna."

I pulled the brush away from the well's opening. The air wiggled in front of Jessica then. It was like on a hot day when heat waves make what you're looking at swirl around.

"Meet Zanna," I said.

Jessica was confused. "Who? What?" I laughed out loud.

"No, Zanna, don't!" I yelled, but it was too late. Zanna moved fast, in a blur. Zanna shoved her and Jessica slid towards the hole. She caught herself at the very edge... Zanna stuck out her hand as if to help. Jessica reached out and grabbed her but Zanna pulled away. Jessica's fingernails dug into Zanna's arm as her final hold slipped away. Cursing, she fell to the bottom with a splat!

Then everything was quiet again.

I started to run away but Jessica started screaming...so loud. I heard her choking on something and Zanna laughed.

"Help...me...Elena!"

Around the edge of the well were some big rocks left from when it was dug years before. They were too heavy for me, but Zanna grabbed one at a time and threw them down the hole. Some made a splatting sound when they hit the mud. Others made a different sound, a hollow sound, followed by Jessica's cries. Zanna laughed until tears ran down her face until finally, the screaming stopped. Oh, how I loved the quiet.

"Poor Jessica," I said.

"It's OK. Mommy will keep her company until we go camping again," Zanna smiled.

I ran back to the cabin and Daddy was sitting at the kitchen table. "What did you do to your arm. Elena? You're bleeding." Dadday said.

"Oh, it's just a little scratch. Zanna said it's a small price to pay."

Daddy looked really worried about me then. "Elena, where is Jessica? What did you do? Please tell me...not again?"

"Jessica had an accident, Daddy. Don't worry, Mommy and Abby will keep her company."

Daddy was so happy that I was safe and we were free of Jessica. He dropped his head in his hands and cried.

"Oh, Elena...Elena..." He kept repeating.

Silly Jessica. She should have known. Daddy and I will always be together. Maybe next year we'll go to the beach.

Forbidden Love

By Erika M Szabo

The mystic runes etched on the ancient stone glimmered in the moonlight, casting an eerie glow on the discarded rubble scattered around it. I heard the whispers of an ancient voice lost in time telling me a story, a tale of a time long forgotten, of the people who had once lived in these lands. As the whispers grew louder, the runes began to glow brighter until they shone like stars in the night sky.

∗∗∗

In medieval times, there lived a young nobleman named Edward. He was the son of the King's advisor and had grown up in the royal palace. Although he had royal blood, Edward was a gentle and kind-hearted young man. His future was planned out by the King, and no matter his objections, Edward was ordered to marry a noblewoman, the King's cousin. He pleaded with his father, but he couldn't advise him to defy the King's order.

As fate would have it, Edward was injured during a hunting trip far from the palace and came across a village seeking medical help. The villagers took him to their healer, a beautiful peasant girl named Marianne.

Seeing Edward's condition, she immediately tended to his wounds. Marianne's mother had passed away when she was young, leaving her to care for her younger siblings and father. Despite her hardships, Marianne was known for her kind nature and ability to heal even the most severe wounds.

In the short time they spent together, Edward and Marianne fell deeply in love. At first, they tried to fight their feelings and ignore their attraction towards each other. But the more they tried to suppress their love, the more it grew. They eventually realized that they needed to be together, even if it meant breaking the societal norms of their time.

However, Edward knew that their love was forbidden. Nobles were not allowed to marry commoners, and he was expected to marry a woman from a prestigious family to solidify his position in society. Despite the odds, Edward was determined to be with Marianne. They couldn't help the way they felt, and their love for each other was too strong to ignore.

They made plans to elope and start a new life together far from the constraints of society. They understood the societal norms and that their relationship would never be accepted. But they couldn't deny the deep love they had for each other. So, they decided to leave their old lives behind and start anew. They were ready to face whatever trials and tribulations that may come their way, for the sake of their love.

While their love was forbidden, it was something worth fighting for. Edward and Marianne were willing to leave everything behind and face the consequences of their actions to be together. Their love was so strong that it motivated them to disobey the norms of society, something that was unheard of during medieval times.

They eloped in secret, which was a risky and daring decision. They knew that their actions would have consequences, but their love for each other was worth it. After exchanging vows in a small chapel, they started a new life together, far away from the royal palace and the expectations of society.

Despite the challenges they faced, they never wavered in their love for each other. They lived together in a small cottage, deep in the woods, and spent their days hunting and tending to their garden, living a simple life filled with love.

This was a peaceful and tranquil place where they could be together free from the expectations of society.

Though Edward and Marianne's love story was filled with love and passion, it ultimately had a tragic end. After several years of living in hiding, their secret was discovered. Despite Edward's pleading, the King sentenced him to life in prison for defying his order to marry a noblewoman. To punish Edward further, with a cruel grin, the King sent Marianne to his bed chamber. She cried and pleaded on her knees, but the King laughed when his servants dragged the devastated woman away.

Edward begged and pleaded to no avail, he was chained and thrown into a dark room in the dungeon.

Marianne couldn't face the dark future awaiting her and hung herself on the bedpost when the servants left the room.

Edward managed to free an arm and reached for the dagger the servants forgot to take from him. He plunged the dagger into his heart.

Their true love and noble deaths shook the community, and their story was passed down through the generations as a tale that spoke of forbidden love and the consequences of going against the order of the King. Though their love wasn't acknowledged by society, it became immortalized as a flame that refused to be extinguished by socially driven conventions. Their love story became a legend, inspiring others to follow their hearts and pursue true love, no matter what obstacles may stand in their way.

***

And then, as suddenly as it had begun, it was over. The wind died down, the whispers faded away, and the runes returned to their silent slumber, waiting for the next traveler to come along and hear their tale.

A Well-kept Home

By Toi Thomas

1952 The Fields Family Farm

The sun was high in the midday sky crisping the surface of the ground in a way that only southern folk knew how to navigate. From the open window of the large, white country estate, on land that used to be a profitable plantation before you had to pay your laborers, the argument between Jericho and Makayla Fields could be heard reverberating across the toasting corn stalks for miles.

Kayla shook her head in defeat. "Why would you do something like this, Daddy? It don't make no sense."

"It makes perfect sense, Kayla. You just don't like it." The old man, older than he should have been for having a 19-year-old daughter, hobbled around the kitchen and settled into the chair at the head of the table. "You always knew it was going to be this way."

"No, Daddy. I didn't know. I didn't know that not having a penis meant I'd be left with nothing once you died."

"Don't talk to me like that. That right there is why stupid girls like you don't run farms. Y'all got no respect."

Kayla stomped her foot on the polished tiled floor. "You want to talk about respect. I've been slaving my ass off taking care of you and this farm ever since mom died and you broke your leg. I didn't go off to college like all my friends so I could help you run this place, while your precious firstborn ran off to chase skirts. The singular reason he'd even be fit to own this farm is because you're stupid enough to give it to him, even after failing out of three schools. Why should I respect you when you clearly don't respect me?"

The old man slammed his fist on the table. "You respect me 'cause I'm your daddy and I say so. This is how it is. I ain't leaving you with nothing. You're gonna get your mommy's China and jewelry. Stop being so selfish."

Kayla took a deep breath and walked past her father in silence. She stomped up the back stairs and headed straight to her room. Her father called after her demanding she come back and say something. The boom of his voice could be heard from any corner of the house and well out into the pastures. Jericho always did enjoy a good argument, sometimes it was a good excuse for him to raise his hands to her, but he soon learned that Kayla wasn't like her mother. She would hit back just as hard as he did. She had made a point to learn how to box and defend herself. Still, he wanted a rise out of her, and she was ignoring him.

At last, she stepped out of her room wearing a stuffed backpack and carrying a shoulder bag. She ran down the hall, down the front staircase, and stood at the front door. "Go to hell, Daddy." She yelled as the old man hobbled out of the kitchen toward the front door. "I mean it from the bottom of my heart when I tell you that you and Junior deserve whatever is coming to you. I won't be around to see it."

She was out the door before he could even take a breath to retort, but it didn't stop him from shouting and yelling anyway. He watched from the open door as she hopped on her bike and peddled away, against the heat of the day and the will of her father. She hadn't bothered taking the car, it didn't belong to her. Nothing around there belonged to her. Kayla had decided she was done with The Fields Family Farm and anything associated with it. The further down the road she traveled, the less she could hear of her father's curses and guilt trips. If she was wrong to leave a crippled old man all by himself, she didn't care.

1962 First Generation Macy Family Realtors

Mary Macy was desperate to make this sale. Business had been steady, but not very profitable, considering she was the first woman of mixed race to own a business in the county. If she could get someone to take The Fields Family Farm off her hands the commission would be enough for her to pay off the last of her debts and just breathe a little easier. Plus, her relatives had gone all in on her starting this real estate firm, and she wanted to make sure they all got a good return on their investments.

Pointing to gleaming polished wood floors, she looked at the excited couple, "So, tell me. What are you two thinking? I know the original floors and hand-crafted molding are to die for."

The man reached for the woman's hand and brought it up to his mouth to kiss before looking at Mary. "It is quite breathtaking, just like my bride." The wife giggled and blushed but said very little.

Mary nodded her head, "Absolutely, you and your lovely bride would do quite well to raise a family in a home like this. They just don't make'm like this anymore."

The couple circled each other a few times pointing out things they liked about the house. At one point, the wife scuffed her shoes on the floor. One second the mark was there, the next it was gone. She flipped her hair and moved on, assuming she'd imagined the mark. The groom asked, "This house has been empty for almost ten years. It seems to be in an incredible condition for its age. Why is it still on the market?"

Mary moved her hands behind her back to conceal how much they were shaking. It always came down to this question. She could lie, but they would find out and be upset that she hadn't told them. She exhaled and smiled wide as she explained, "Yes, the house has been empty for quite a while, but it hasn't been on the market that long. Because you're likely to hear rumors elsewhere, I'll tell you the truth of what I know upfront."

Before she could utter another word, the wind whistled outside, and the wife jerked her head toward the large bay window looking out on what used to be corn fields. Fall leaves danced in a tiny whirlwind. "Did someone die in this house?"

Mary sighed, "Yes, but only of old age." *They don't need to know about the son right now, besides, that was an accident.* "There's been no evidence of anything remotely fowl. This is called The Fields Family Farm for a reason. The Fields family lived here for generations, but they've all died off now."

She could see the couple's shoulders sinking in relief at her explanation. Feeling encouraged by their body language she went on. "You could of course rename the land if you decide to take it on. In any case, after the father and son passed away, there was said to be a daughter who'd inherited everything by default, but several years went by without her ever coming around to claim it. Eventually, the state took it and contracted my firm to sell it."

The man rubbed soft circles into his wife's back as he responded to Mary's explanation. "That doesn't seem so bad. There must be more to it. We are definitely interested but we want to make sure we're not walking into a trap." The lights in the house dimmed. It was so subtle, that neither the couple nor the realtor noticed it.

Forcing herself not to cross her arms, Mary pursed her lips. "I appreciate your candidness, but there's no trap here. That's not how I do business. I think this is a great property for a young wealthy couple looking to start a family. If you don't let rumors of lost heiresses, no longer with a claim to the land, bother you, it's possible you could be happy here."

The couple clinched their hands together and embraced as they walked toward the large staircase in the main hall. They looked up and then looked at each other and smiled. The man called out to Mary without looking at her, "We'll take it."

Mary began to tear up in relief as she felt a breeze sweep by. She turned toward the bay window. It was not open nor was the front door. This was an old house, and despite its impeccable condition, old houses were prone to odd wisps of wind. She shrugged her shoulders. *Maybe the house is relieved to finally have an owner after all these years.*

1972 The Home for Squatters

With the southern humidity bringing spurts of rain every half hour, two homeless young travelers needed a place of refuge. On the outside, the pristine country estate looked like a monument to a time long passed. On the inside, the squatters reveled in the comfort of a hidden gem.

"How'd you find this place, man?" Stevey dropped to his knees before laying flat and log-rolling on the floor.

Stiles turned to his half-baked friend and rolled him onto a blanket- one of many fabrics he was hanging over windows and laying out across the floors. "Come on, Stevey, stay off the floors. I told you this is just temporary. Someone will come to check on this place, soon enough, and we can't leave any traces."

Stevey sat up on the blanket and held a soda bottle in his arms like a baby. "Yeah, you're right. We gotta be careful, but seriously, how did you find this place? It looks too good to be abandoned."

Stiles finished hanging the sheets over the last of the windows before joining his friend on the blankets. He pulled out a half-smoked joint, relit it, and puffed two times before passing it on. "I hitched a ride out to that lake, just up the road, a few weeks ago. I heard some of those rich folks talking about some couple who'd had enough of country life and decided to move their kids to the city."

"Wow, rich people are crazy." The friends passed the small joint between them until it was gone. Stevey opened his soda and took a swig. "How could you just walk away from all this? This place is so clean and nice, and warm. This is probably the warmest place we've ever laid up in."

"I know. I couldn't believe it when I saw it. I followed a bunch of them up from the lake…" Stiles took off his hoodie and used it to prop up his head as he leaned onto the wall. "They were hiking up to those new cabins at the end of the road. I don't know why rich people like hiking so much. When we do it it's called wandering but when they do it, it's hiking."

"And then what," asked Stevey before letting out a loud belch. "Did you just walk right in?"

Stiles turned to his friend and smirked. "Actually, I did. No one was interested in coming down the long road from the cabins to get here. It was easy for me to move around without being seen. The key was stupidly under the mat."

The two friends laughed and shook their heads when they heard the faint sound of another person laughing. They both stopped and jumped to their feet. They stood back-to-back and jerked their heads around as their eyes surveyed and ears stretched to hear the sound again. After a few moments, they began to relax.

Stiles gulped. "I'm sure it was just a group of hikers passing by too close."

Stevey shook his head in agreement. The two friends walked towards the windows, pulled back the fabric, and looked out into the star-scattered night. The moon was bright, but the woods were dark. They wouldn't be able to see anyone moving through the area unless they were shining a light.

Back on the blankets, the two friends sat back-to-back, each munching on a preferred snack food. Stiles was the first to break the silence. "Ya know, I wonder if this is that haunted house people be sometimes talking about in town?"

Stevey jerked his head to the side, staring daggers in his periphery towards Stiles, "Great, you found us a haunted house to crash in. No wonder it was so easy to get into."

"I never said it was haunted. I just said I wonder if it is. I heard people saying some bodies had been found a while back in one of these fancy houses."

"Man, you didn't say anything about bodies earlier."

Stiles huffed, "Well, I didn't think about it earlier, but it's not that bad. Apparently, some old guys on the run from the law fell asleep and didn't wake up."

Stevey began to whine, "I don't want to fall asleep and never wake up."

Stiles turned and patted his friend on the shoulder. "You won't. We'll be safe here. We're not old and we're not wanted. Who knows what really happened to those guys, besides, if that rich couple could have kids here, it can't be that bad."

Stiles and Stevey decided to call it a night, turning off lights and checking all the rooms to make sure no one else was there. After gathering their items in the main room to sleep, Stevey put a fresh pair of batteries into a flashlight and left it lit in the hallway. Stiles watched the action and nodded in agreement before they went to sleep without another word, laying back-to-back on their pile of blankets.

1982 Second Generation Macy Family Realtors

Nancy was determined to be the next big thing in real estate. She'd do her mother proud. They had now established a long-standing tradition in the area. Everyone knew the Macy Family Realtors were the ones who could sell any property and make everyone happy at the end of the day. Her mother was still in the field, along with a rainbow of aunts and cousins, who were all dealing with high-profile cases. She and the new hires were given grunt work and "throw-away" cases that no one stressed about finalizing. She'd stumbled across a problem property and decided this would be the way she'd make a name for herself.

On her day off, she drove out to the Fields Family Farm, also known as the Failed Estate. After the Macys had acquired the contract from the state to sell the house and land, her mother found the perfect young couple to take it over. Still, it wasn't long after they had their first child, that the rumors of strange goings on began to spread. The couple left the house after three years. Nancy stood at the bottom of the steps leading up to the front door and shook her head. She hugged herself against the chill in the winter air. *How can this place be 30 years old? It looks brand new. Who's been coming by and keeping this place up?*

Nancy ascended the stairs and used a master key to open the padlock and release the chain around the door. For years, the company had struggled to sell the property to another buyer, often having to chase away squatters. The padlock and floodlights were new editions to help cut down on what her mom called "riff-raff."

A variety of homeless wanderers had lived in the house over the years, even a single mom with two young boys. However, when she and her sons were ultimately discovered, people in town rallied around them and helped her get a job and a small apartment in town. To this day, she swears life was easier on the estate. She'd say, "The house practically took care of itself and sometimes me too."

Making her way into the front room and ignoring the sound of creeks in the floor some might think were footsteps- Nancy wasn't fazed. She knew what old houses sounded like. Staring out the bay window, looking out on a flat frosted field, she remembered being about the same age as the little boys when the mom had been discovered. She was there with her mom that day, along with the sheriff and a bunch of other government officials, to help the boys feel safe around all the adults. Nancy supposed it worked out for the best since the woman and her boys moved in with her new husband a few years later, just as happy as they could be.

Nancy toured the entire house, making note of the astonishing condition. The floors appeared to be polished, the molding was cobweb-free, and all the light fixtures were in good working order. She stood in the kitchen admiring the combination of old and new appliances- the retro-modern style of the decor. It was the best of 1950's luxury and 1980s convenience. She sat for a moment at the nook table, an apparent original antique that belonged to the Fields.

She tapped her foot on the floor, listening to the sound echo down the hall and even up the back staircase. After a few moments, the seat of the chair felt warm under her bottom. She stood and turned to feel the surface with her hand, but it was cool to the touch. She sat in the next chair to the right and after a few minutes, she hadn't noticed any temperature change. She shrugged her shoulders and then stood to survey the land around the house.

She stepped out the back door, down the wooden staircase, and onto the path that snaked around the exterior, all along the flower beds, which of course, appeared to be well maintained even in the dead of winter. Nancy knew the realtor group didn't pay for grounds maintenance on properties this far out into the country and made a note to look into how much the company was spending on maintenance. If she could sell this place, it would do more than make a name for her, it could boost the company to expand in the commercial industry.

Nancy stood at the edge of the yard, where the slumbering grass met the gravel path leading to the old barn. She looked out over the flat land. It looked so bear with no crops filling the space. Walking towards the barn, she heard a whisper in the air. "Don't enter if you don't plan to work it." Nancy whirled around. No one was there. She took a few more steps towards the barn, "Be mindful of your actions."

Nancy's eyes bulged and her pawns began to sweat. "Who's there? Y'all ain't supposed to be squatt'n around here. I will call the sheriff if I need to!" But there was no reply. She looked and turned and looked some more.

She took a step back and sighed and the wind replied, "There, there now."

Nancy returned to her vehicle a little shaken but still determined. *Maybe there's more to why we haven't sold this place, but I'm still going to make this happen.*

1992 The Dabneys

Nancy met the deputy at the end of the driveway. She could tell he was one of the new recruits- she didn't know him, and he didn't know her. He checked her identification and spoke into the walkie over his shoulder. Nancy shook her head and sighed. *I really thought it was going to work this time. The third time is supposed to be the charm.*

Nancy looked around at the scene. Everything was taped off and one of the ambulances was pulling away. The other was still sitting idle as Mrs. Dabney sat, strapped to one of those rolling beds, while she sobbed into a towel, soaked with her husband's blood. The bruise on her cheek was too red to be concealed.

Nancy was given the go-ahead to speak with her client and friend before she was taken to the hospital. "Evening Gail, I sure hate to see you like this. Guess you all won't be having me over for dinner this weekend."

Gail looked up and blinked away a few tears before she gulped in air, forcing her sobs to cease. "I'm so sorry, Nancy. I know you tried to help me, but I was too stubborn to admit what was going on."

Nancy reached for her cheek but decided better and instead took Gail's free hand and squeezed it. "Don't you dare apologize. When I sold y'all this place, I did so because I thought you all would fill it with love. Not yells and screams."

Gail Dabney removed the towel from her face and stared at Nancy. "You know, none of this is my blood. It's his. I only have the red cheek-"

Nancy cut her off, "This time. But you and I both know, there have been other bruises and scars."

"I tried to get help so many times, but I couldn't do it. This time, I called the police but then…" Gail looked around, making sure no one was too close to listen in. "She just couldn't take it anymore."

Nancy reached over and grabbed Gail's other hand. "Who couldn't take it? Was there someone else here?"

Gail laughed. "That's funny, Nancy. Like you don't know who I'm talking about. You warned us that the house would look after us as long as we looked after it. I guess she doesn't stand for wife beat'n."

"What are you saying, Gail? You think the house killed Richard."

"How else did he fall down the stairs? I was hiding in the pantry on the phone with 9-1-1 when it happened. And he wasn't a clumsy man."

Nancy tried to take a step back, but Gail held firm to her hands. "Honey, I get that you may be experiencing a litany of emotions right now, but I don't think the house is responsible. He just slipped. Serves him right if you ask me. If he hadn't been coming after you like that, maybe he'd still be alive."

Gail ripped her hands away from Nancy. "Don't patronize me, Nancy. Not you. You and your mother know how special this place is. The reason I came out of hiding was to see why he had stopped yelling, and there he was. Bleeding at the bottom of the stairs, while the steps were settling themselves back into place, like nothing had happened." Gail nodded in a matter-of-fact way.

Nancy's jaw dropped in an attempt to respond, but just then the deputy approached and announced, "It's time for you to head off to the hospital Mrs. Dabney. The sheriff and your lawyer will meet you there." EMTs came and closed the door of the ambulance and went up front to start the vehicle.

Nancy stared at Gail through the window as she continued to wipe her face with the bloodied towel. She shook her head and then turned to look at the house. There were people buzzing all around the exterior but to look inside through the windows, the house seemed empty and serene.

2002 The Journalist

No one was interested in the story of an old house that was on and off the market as much as a young pop star on the dating scene, but Lewis knew there was a story worth telling buried in the county records. He'd already made a name for himself, not only as a black man in a field many weren't expecting to see him in, but in larger cities he was known as the man cracking cold cases wide open. Now, he was working his way across the country seeking more historical mysteries to solve.

On his way to a fishing trip with some friends, he heard a brief story about the Failed Estate and was intrigued. He cut his trip short and headed north, from the gulf. He knew better than to let the locals know what he was doing in town right away. Smalltown folk were either uncomfortably friendly or brutally unfriendly, there was no in-between. With his press credentials in tow, he booked a room at the inn at the center of the quaint town, though just a few miles outside of town, the area was built up like any typical commerce district. There were several chain restaurants, both a strip mall and an indoor mall with anything you could want to buy, and an array of common motel and hotel options.

Lewis liked to be close to his subjects. He felt it made it easier to pack up and leave if his things were nearby. For anyone who asked, he started out telling people that he was doing research on Civil War-era architecture, which was a partial truth. A few Google searches before he started his trip told him that the Failed Este was a house that used to be owned by a wealthy family that made their money with a slave plantation.

The story was that after the slaves were free, the remaining three sons of the landowner fought over how to run and manage things until two of them sold their shares of the land to their oldest brother before leaving the area never to return. According to the courthouse records, there are no surviving members of the original Fields. The two brothers moved away and started families. One of them and their family died in an earthquake out west and the other lost his wife in a tragic fire before they had any kids.

Jericho Fields- the great-grandson of the oldest brother, his wife, and their two children were left to run the plantation, down-sized to a residential farm, after much of the land was sold to the government. For years, the family farm thrived with the aid of hired hands. When the mother died of a mysterious fever, the two kids became regular fixtures on the farm until the son went away to college. When the daughter was 17 years old, records indicate that she was placed in a managerial position over the day-to-day running of the business while attending night school for a degree. She was accredited with earning the farm several awards and making many improvements to upgrade farm equipment and practices.

Then one day, Makayla Fields, the ambitious daughter, disappeared. According to public records, Mr. Fields had left the entire farm and business to his son, leaving the daughter with some life insurance money, a China set, and some jewelry. Old newspapers, however, reported on the day of the funeral the daughter was nowhere to be found. Then about a month after burying his father, Jonathan Fields died, slipping in the tub and hitting his head. One of the farmhands found him. Again, at the brother's funeral, Makayla Fields was nowhere to be found. Legally, the farm and house belonged to her as the sole surviving member of the family, but she never surfaced to claim it.

After gathering details on the original owners of the house, Lewis began to look into the claims regarding the estate being haunted. He wanted to know why people thought it was "possessed", as there were no reported ghost sightings in this area on the usual paranormal outlets. He was also curious to learn who or what was supposedly haunting the house.

Posing as a potential buyer, looking to set up a small research museum, Lewis was able to have a young member of the Macy Family Realtors show him the property. It had taken three days for his request to be granted. Lately, that had become quite a problem for the real estate group- people wanting tours of the estate with no intention to buy it. Everyone just wanted to see the "haunted" Failed Estate.

When they arrived at the property, the young woman- the grandniece of Mary Macy, cursed under her breath. It was a sunny warm day, but it had rained the day before and the ground was wet. Sandy pulled out a box of shoe coverings and directed Lewis to follow her up the stairs to the front door. She entered the code into the keypad and opened the door wide, swinging out her arm to block Lewis from entering right away.

"You gotta put this on first, sir." She took out a pair of blue paper covers and then handed him the box.

"Of course," Lewis replied before pulling out a pair for himself.

With their shoes covered, Sandy placed the box on the porch, off to the side of the door, so it didn't block the doorway. Then she exhaled and rang the doorbell.

Lewis questioned, "You expecting someone to be home?'

Sandy sighed, "I don't know how they get in with all the doors and windows locked, but sometimes there are people just hanging out in here."

After waiting a few moments more, she stepped into the house and motioned for Lewis to follow her. The house was more immaculate than the rumors had suggested. As they traversed the long hallways, stairs, original wood, and tile floors, the realtor rattled off facts about the place, like a high school student preparing for a history test.

Lewis turned to interrupt. "Look, I can see this is not ideal for you so let's just get down to it."

Sandy crossed her arms and cut him off from saying anything else. "I don't know anything about this place being haunted and if you try anything, there's a deputy waiting out in the woods ready to back me up. We know how these things work around here now."

Lewis lifted both his hands in a surrendering gesture. "Ok, good to know about the deputy. Why don't we just head back and call it a day?"

Without speaking another word, Sandy stomped her foot and turned on her hills. She turned off lights and closed doors as they exited the house. On the car ride back to the realtor's office, she apologized. "I'm sorry I snapped at you, but I just assume you are another one of those ghost hunters."

"It's okay. We do live in strange times, and you don't know me." Again, lifting his hands in a gesture to convey a non-threat, he explained. "Some people consider all historians to be ghost hunters because we're always more interested in the past than the present."

She looked at him out of the corner of her eye as she drove. "Are you really a historian?"

"Yes, I am, but I don't work for a museum. I'm a journalist."

Sandy smiled, "Well, you're probably gonna write whatever story you want to anyway, so I'll tell you something off the record." She took her eyes off the road for a split second, snapped her head at him, and mentally shot lightning his way before refocusing on the road. "Ask me to say any of this in public and I'll say you're nuts."

Lewis laughed. "Fair enough. What do you want to tell me?"

"I think it's the daughter. They never found her; you know."

Lewis tilted his head. "How could it be her? She was never reported to be seen near the death of her father or her brother. She never came back to claim the land."

Turning into the parking lot, Sandy nodded her head. "That's right, she was never seen, but that don't mean she didn't come home."

"You think she came back and somehow died in the house so she could haunt it?"

Sandy smirked, "When you say it like that it sounds koo koo, but that's not what I'm saying." Lewis nodded his head as to say go on and Sandy explained as they stepped out of the car. They walked close to one another back into the office. "I think she came home for her daddy's funeral and the brother killed her 'cause he felt threatened by her. Everyone knew he was dumb as rocks and his daddy left him everything because he was a sexist bastard."

They stopped at the door and Lewis reached out his hand to open it for Sandy. "That is quite a theory. Why haven't I heard it before?"

Sandy stepped through the door and winked, "Obviously, you've been asking the wrong people." Sandy agreed to have dinner with Lewis that evening and gave him some ideas about who he might want to talk to.

Lewis was able to find listings for two of the previous tenants of the house. One, a mother of two, went on and on about how the house had such a feminine and nurturing ora to it. She always worried that she wasn't doing enough to look after her boys when they were younger, but she said she felt safe leaving the boys in that house alone when she was too poor for childcare and desperate for any work she could find.

Another woman- a widow who was in the process of planning the wedding to her next husband, had a different opinion of the house. Her name was Gail and she always referred to the house as "she". She explained that "I never felt unsafe in the house, but I was always concerned about miss treating her. I never would have won any awards for my domestic skills before living there."

Gail went on for a while about how she would try to clean the house during the day when her husband went to work because he was a hitter. One day she fell asleep trying to wax the floors and when she woke up, the floors were done. She ended their call by stating, "I knew from that moment it wasn't her I was afraid of. She was looking after me the whole time."

2012 Third Generation Macy Family Realtors

Sandy was the first member of the Macy Family Realtors to step away from the company without reaching retirement. She and her husband Lewis had made quite a fuss in town after he published an article explaining what he thought the source of the Failed Estate was. People didn't like being accused of perpetuating rumors in order to boost commerce, but that was the best explanation Lewis felt comfortable printing.

Sandy had defended his choice to spin the tale in the way he did, but everyone was still upset. No one was willing to come forth and corroborate the claims that town folk had been keeping up the estate for years. In fact, many began to rally around the theory Lewis presented in his article that Makayla Fields may have returned home but died before she could claim the land instead of just disappearing.

Sandy was heartbroken when an outpouring of complaints came in for her to be fired from the real estate group as a petition circulated to have the cold case of Kayla's missing person's file reopened. After ten years of pleading and building up notoriety on the Internet, the case was reopened. Lewis did his part to aid local law enforcement with the investigation and in turn, towns folk began to loosen their grudge against him and Sandy.

When the grounds of the estate were tested for human remains, evidence was collected that suggested that a body had been buried under the basement floor at some point. For weeks, crew after crew tried to break up the floor to extract the bones, but something would always impede progress. Drills would break, electrical systems would short out, tools would go missing, personnel would become suddenly ill after having been on the farm the day before, and more.

It was Sandy who came up with a plan to discover who or what was buried in the basement, but first it was going to require an apology. She and Lewis wrote a letter to the town and had it published in the local paper. Of course, nothing stays local these days, so most people online who'd been following the aftermath of Lewis's article saw the letter. In the end, they apologized for their accusations and expressed that there may be forces at play that they do not know or comprehend.

After the letter was published, Sandy gathered the women of the Macy Family Realtor Group and a handful of women of various ages whose bloodlines went back generations in this area. It took a few days, but other previous female tenants of the Failed Estate also arrived to lend their support. There were several women whose families had squatted in the home during tough times over the ages including the mother of the two boys- now grown with kids of their own. There were three granddaughters of the first couple to buy the home from the real estate group. Even the former Mrs. Dabney- now Mrs. Jones came and reconnected with her old friend Nancy Macy, gathered there with her kin.

All the women gathered in the basement, along with the only two women in the surrounding five counties who could operate the drilling equipment. Sandy and the Macy clan went in first followed by the others. They each took a turn telling stories about love and grief and memories associated with the town, Fields Family Farm, and the house they now stood in. After all that, Sandy stepped forward and addressed the house.

"Not everyone here is in agreement about whether ghosts are real or not, but we all feel there is a spirit in need here. We believe this spirit has attached itself to this house and we believe it is the spirit of Makayla Fields." The floor rumbled beneath their feet. Everyone looked around unsure if they should continue or cut their losses.

Sandy continued to speak. "Kayla, we are here to set you free. We're not here to take your spirit from this place, but to give you the proper burial you never had." Air began to whistle in the pipes, creating an uncomfortable screech, but Sandy continued. "We, all here, love you and appreciate you for all you've done over the years and the decades. This is your house, and you are welcome to stay, but we ask that you allow us to exhume your body."

After a short pause, the air in the pipes settled and the floor stopped rumbling. Everyone exhaled at once. One by one they all stepped out of the basement except the two drillers and Sandy, wearing a hard hat and staying out of the way. Once the initial surface of the concrete was broken, it was easy to see the remains of a body were present.

Female deputies from the surrounding counties, one sheriff, and a corner's assistant took over the scene in the basement to ensure the integrity of the extraction and the pending cold case results. Two months later, an all-female construction crew went to install new concrete flooring in the basement of the Makayla Fields Historical Farmhouse.

2022 The Makayla Fields Historical Farm

The hobby farm had made quite a name for itself in the past few years. Few people even remembered the old ghost rumors, yet no one could forget about Kayla with her mausoleum directly out front to greet visitors. The land and, as always, the house were alive again with activity. It had become a cultural center over the years, with Farmer's Markets on the first weekend of the month, weddings on Saturdays, the petting zoo and hayrides on Sundays, and the farming co-op throughout the week.

The co-op was the real bread and butter of the new-old farm. It was a training program for young farmers who came and worked the land, while staying in the main house, to prepare themselves for running their own farms. Every six months, a new crop of young farmers would settle in on the second floor of the estate, after a drinking contest granted one lucky participant access to the master suite. The other four tenants would have to share the other rooms with their adjoining bathrooms.

Peter was the king of the master suite for the time being, but he was very gracious to offer up his bathroom space whenever things were tight- five manual laboring adults sharing three bathrooms is a feat no matter how you split it. Always the earliest to rise, Peter would be up in the barn greasing down equipment before it was time to start feeding the animals.

With the full backing of the local community, the farm was under no pressure to sustain itself and received most of its revenue from the events held there, so practicing farmers like Peter could learn at their own pace and not be afraid to test and try out new things. With the farmers in training taking care of the day-to-day tasks, of feeding and looking after the petting zoo animals, tending to the small crops of vegetable and seasonal flowers, and learning to use and maintain farm equipment, the added benefit of a full-time cook made this co-op more valuable than one might assume.

Every morning the cook would arrive, with the moon shining outside, to have breakfast ready. All three daily meals were served on strict schedules, and by 4:00 p.m. the cook was heading home for the day. There was always something available to snack on in the kitchen for anyone wanting something warmed or chilled later in the evening. Still, the most enticing feature of the Kayla Fields Historical "hobby" Farm that had applicants from around the world clambering to spend six months of their lives, putting in long hours with no pay but some good food, was Kayla herself.

Peter wanted to be the first of this group to see her. It was something the everyday tourist didn't know about but in the farming world, it was all the buzz. Kayla was still working her farm. She had, according to some, been spotted, sweeping the barn floor, feeding pigs, and brushing the main of a donkey. No one had ever said anything about her being seen in the house, though her presence could clearly be felt. Throughout the decades, the house continued to maintain its impeccable condition, but Peter was singularly focused. He spent a lot of time in the barn hoping to see her there.

One night, in a minor bout of insomnia, Peter decided to explore parts of the house and land he had been too busy to discover during the normal working day. He inspected Kayla's mausoleum, being careful not to disturb anything while leaving a single tulip behind. They were grown in a greenhouse behind the barn just so they'd always be on hand anytime someone wanted to visit Kayla.

Then he wandered the ground to the point where the gravel road met the main paved road. He turned around and walked the land until it turned marshy- leading up to the lake. He then turned back, still not tired enough to sleep, and focused his attention on the house. Already familiar with the second floor, he decided to explore the rooms on the first level.

He headed in through the back door connected to the kitchen, and instead of going straight up the staircase as usual, he walked down the long narrow hall. The bathroom on this level was rarely used by the tenants as a courtesy to the cook when she was on the premises. Beyond that, he stepped into the mahogany-lined study for the first time. He knew it was there but hadn't had a reason to venture in before now. Though it was called a study, it looked more like a small library with two large built-in desks. The space was told to be very popular amongst the high school crowd as a place for their senior pictures to be taken.

Then he ventured into the tearoom. Pink came to mind before he stepped in and realized it was decorated in pastels of many colors, not just pink. It was a small den-like area with a rolling tea tray, ready to serve whatever intimate events occurred in the space: book clubs, engagement parties, and gender reveals.

Peter passed the door to the dining room and walked a little further to enter the main living area, which connected to the dining room with pocket doors. The main living area had a reputation of its own. The main wall was filled with pictures of people who'd taken selfies in the bay window looking over the flower garden, a much smaller space than the cornfield that used to be there. All the furniture was antique but restored from the local area and fit perfectly in place on the original wood floors that always creaked at just the right moment. The pocket doors were open putting the grand table and chairs of the dining room on display.

Standing in the hall, in front of the front door, Peter studied the space. *Have I seen everything? I feel like there's something I'm missing.* He peered down the dark hall, beyond the large staircase, as the light from the hall chandelier faded and he took notice of a nondescript, almost invisible, door next to the cook's bathroom. He approached the door, hesitated, and then reached out his hand to touch the knob. It was cold, ice cold to the touch. *I'm on to something.*

He stepped into a small closet, a sort of utility room with another door marked, in large red letters, with caution. "Basement level. No men allowed." Peter took out his phone and began to record.

"I'm about to do something stupid, but I just can't seem to help myself. I want to see Kayla and I think she's down in this basement. Here I go." He placed his hand on the knob of the door leading to the basement. It was hot, and yet, he turned the knob and entered the space.

Peter was happy to be alive as he packed the last of his things. He waited, taking sad slow breaths, for an escort down the hall and down the stairs to exit the house to never return. His dreams of running his own farm may be shattered but there was still a chance he could do some things, due to all the advancements in technology and modified equipment now available.

Once he stepped out of the house, the doors closed behind him. No one had spoken to him since he'd been found in the basement. The silent treatment he received over the last two weeks was the toughest part of his trauma. No one wanted to hear his story. Whenever he tried to tell someone what happened to him, they would turn away.

Peter shed a tear as his taxi drove away, carrying him to the airport. He'd wanted to look upon the glory of The Makayla Fields Historical Farm one more time but being blind kept that from happening. Maybe one day, he'd have a chance to tell someone what the last thing he saw really was. For now, he was an example. No one would challenge Kayla again and no man would ever again step foot in the basement of her house.

Don't Whistle Back

By Erika M Szabo

Milena, a young teenager with chocolate brown eyes and long black hair, hadn't seen her grandfather in over a year who lived in Mexico all alone since her grandmother passed away a year ago. The thought of her grandmother filled her with sadness. She remembered the happy visits to their farm when she was younger, and how much joy and love filled her memories of the times she spent with them.

The old farmhouse of her grandparents was nothing like their small apartment in New York. The only vegetation she could see in the concrete jungle neighborhood were a few flowerpots in windows and a sickly, old maple tree at the end of the dead-end road. Since she was a small child, she often told her parents that she wanted to live in Mexico, and her parents promised to move back when they saved enough money to modernize her grandfather's farm.

"I have big plans, but we can't run a successful farm without modern equipment," her father, Alejandro explained. "And we can't make enough money in Mexico to buy them. We have good jobs here, and I promise that as soon as we have enough money saved, we'll move back."

***

As her father drove their beat-up station wagon, Milena admired the beauty of the countryside. The fields were filled with tall, golden grass, swaying gently in the warm breeze. In the distance, she could see the peaks of the mountains, their jagged edges reaching up to touch the sky.

As soon as they arrived and her father parked the car, Milena ran up to the front porch, where her grandfather was sitting in an old rocking chair. His warm smile displayed his brownish-colored teeth from decades of pipe smoking.

"Abuelo!" Milena shouted, her voice trembling with emotion. "It's so good to see you again."

Pedro hugged them and invited them in. Milena noticed a peculiar rope with seven knots hanging by the front door. "Why did you hang that rope there?" she asked her grandfather.

The round-faced man with wrinkled, sunbaked skin, shrugged. "It's just… it's nothing," he hesitantly replied and went inside.

After they settled down and finished lunch, her parents and grandfather sat in rocking chairs on the porch, talking. Milena was too excited to sit still. "I'm going for a walk," she announced.

Her mother, Maria, nodded, smiled, and watched her daughter skipping down the steps and running with outstretched arms.

Milena ran until her legs got tired. She kicked off her boots and lay in the lush grass, looking up at the sky and wiggling her bare toes. She closed her eyes and let the warm sun wash over her, soaking up the tranquil atmosphere. She could hear the birds singing and the distant sound of cows mooing in the nearby fields.

But then, suddenly, a mesmerizing melody filled her ears. Someone was whistling nearby. It was a charming tune with an otherworldly sound to it. She sat up and looked around, expecting to see someone, but there was nobody nearby except the chickens feasting on bugs and cows grazing in the distance.

Her heartbeat quickened and slowly looked around the field, eyes darting from side to side. She was alone far from the house, there weren't any other people in sight. So, she drew a deep breath and then whistled the tune. As she heard a whistle in response, her eyes widened, and a cold chill ran up her spine. The melody didn't sound appealing anymore, it sounded frightening. The young girl jumped up and ran towards the house, leaving her boots behind.

Her bare feet were torn up by twigs and rocks, but she didn't dare to stop. With the house in sight, she saw her parents and grandfather rushing down the steps of the front porch toward her and heard them yelling and waving their arms.

Suddenly, she felt strong, feathered wings grabbing her shoulders and when she turned her head and looked up, she shrunk back in repulsion. She saw an old woman's face, but her arms and shoulders were covered with black feathers. Her face was lined with deep wrinkles and her lips dry and cracked. Milena smelled a foul stench emitting from the woman's mouth, who embraced her with her huge wings and started dragging her away.

Milena screamed in fright and tried to wiggle out of the strong clinch of the woman's wings when she heard running footsteps and her grandfather's shout. "Let her go, La Lechusa!"

Milena turned and saw her grandfather throwing a handful of powdery substances into the woman's face. The young girl teared up, coughed, and sneezed, tasting salty chili powder on her tongue.

The woman's body shook, she sneezed and howled, but let the young girl go. Milena fell and watched the old woman spread her wings and kick off the ground flying away.

Alejandro rushed over and carried Milena inside the house. As her mom hugged her tightly and cooed in her ears to calm her, Milena told her family what happened. "I heard someone whistling a melody, and I whistled back," she sobbed. "And then, she grabbed me and tried to take me away. Who is she? Why is she dressed in feathers, and… how can she fly?" she questions her grandfather, sobbing.

"You summoned La Lechusa," he explained. "She's a bruja, a witch with mystical powers. She could shapeshift into an owl. That's how she finds prey. She whistles a tune and if you whistle back… She can also lure her targets, often children or drunk people, out of houses by crying like a baby or by swooping down on people late at night."

"Papá!" Maria cried out. "It's just silly folklore."

"Is it?" Pedro asked. "Didn't you just see her fly away with your own eyes?"

Maria drew a sharp breath. "I think I did, but…" she mumbled turning away.

"She will come back tonight…" Pedro said, looking at his son-in-law, scratching his chin. "We better get ready for her. She can't enter the house, so Maria and Milena will be safe. We'll wait for her on the porch. I'll get the guns."

"Are you sure she can't come into the house?" Maria asked, her voice trembling in fear.

"I'm sure," Pedro replied. "I hung the rope by the door, that keeps her away."

Milena knew why her grandfather didn't answer her question about the seven knots on the rope. He knew they wouldn't believe him. But now… The night was still and quiet. Milena huddled under the warm cover with Maria. They were anxious and afraid, listening to every sound. And then they heard it.

The whistled tune grew louder and louder. Milena crept to the window, Maria right behind her. Peering outside, they saw a massive black owl hovering outside the window. It had an old woman's face and it whistled through puckered lips. Milena felt a strong urge and threw her hands over her mouth, knowing she must not whistle back.

The sound of a shotgun made them jump in fright. The huge bird with an old woman's face dropped to the ground, with an obvious injury to its left wing, but shook her body and flew off into the night. Milena saw her grandfather standing on the porch with a shotgun. Next to him stood her father. She shook as she listened to them bicker. Her father asked, "Why didn't you just kill the darn thing?"

Pedro calmly said, "Because if you kill La Lechusa, you will die. If you injure her, she will stay away from your house, forever."

The following morning seemed to wash away all the terror of the night. The smell of the feast Milena's mother prepared filled the house.

To this day, the legend of La Lechusa lives on, daring no one to whistle her melody back.

J.A.C.K.S.

(Joint Advanced Command Knowledge System)
A book from the Gospels of Artificial Super
Intelligent Network Manager

By R. A. "Doc" Correa

Definitions:

Cadidiots – J.A.C.K.S. slang for cadets

Cromags – J.A.C.K.S. slang for officers that have not been upgraded to J.A.C.K.S.

Potens – potential candidate for the J.A.C.K.S. program

And the shapes of the locusts were like unto horses prepared unto battle; and on their heads were as it were crowns like gold, and their faces were as the faces of men.

Revelations 9:7 King James Version

May 28, 2073, Eastern slopes of the Sierra Morena, Spain

We exist to serve.

With that thought, Colonel Mark Andrew Gray opens his eyes, doing regulation stretches while waiting for the "coffin" lid to rotate off the tube so he can climb out. Finally exiting the rejuvenation compartment, he passes through the command and troop compartments to the deployment deck, immediately toggling the switch by the hatch to lower the troop ramp.

He dives into mundane ritual, trying to clear his mind of a waking vision. An unfamiliar young blond woman in a third lieutenant's uniform. *Where did that come from?* Trying to shake off the feeling that it's somehow important doesn't improve his mood.

Being disgusted and annoyed is his normal reaction when a new group of West Point cadets are assigned. This time is particularly grating; he's about to start a critical operation. He's not in need of the distraction of "cherry" third louies, though he knows this is S.O.P. After the cadets finish their first year, the final prerequisite for their advancement to a second and final year at the academy is evaluation under field conditions by a senior officer. But inserting these cadidiots into the division at this time? Reckless. *What the hell is wrong with HQ sending these idiots to me at this time. Is there a functional brain cell anywhere in the Pentagon?* Breathing deeply, he reminds himself the J.A.C.K.S. only hold junior to mid-level positions at the "main office"; all the general officers are still cromags, which has him wondering when those dinosaurs will die off.

He leaves the command carrier, walking to the LZ. Within minutes, he sees the stealth VTOL approaching. The UV-123, commonly called "the locust", was developed for the rapid insertion of Mk-17D Cyborg Combat Units into action. Heavily armed and armored, whisper quiet, these craft have been the mainstay of the US Army's rapid lift teams, supporting the main battle force for five years.

It galls him that instead of additional elements, this bird is bringing him half a dozen inexperienced, brain-dead dweebs to nursemaid. Snorting to himself, he hides a grimace behind a stoic mask. They'll be totally useless at this critical time.

The locust flares, dropping hot onto the LZ. The crew chief, a Mk-4H cyborg, shoves the proto shave-tails and their gear off its craft without ceremony. The locust zips back into the sky in a flash, rapidly disappearing over a hill. The entire operation takes less than forty seconds. Impressive.

The colonel loves that kind of efficiency, it has him almost smiling.

It takes nearly five minutes for his new headaches to gather their gear and hightail it over to him. On arrival, they all snap to attention and salute.

Instantly annoyed, Colonel Gray shouts, "What the hell is wrong with you idiots! Are you trying to get us all killed? A single "yard" sniper could nail all of us in less time than I'm taking to yell at you. Get your asses into the carrier while you still *have* asses!"

He chuckles to himself as the new crop of morons scramble into the carrier, tripping over each other and their gear, thinking, *I'm glad I wasn't that much of an idiot when I was a cadet. Don't they teach these kids anything at the Point?*

The M-73A3 Heavy Assault and Command Carrier is designed to provide all command and control for the 82nd ABN Div Cyborg. There are two of these carriers in the division, one for Colonel Gray and his staff, and one for his second in command and her staff. Mustering 5,328 Mk-17D infantry cyborgs, 870 Mk-4H air/vehicle/security/medical crew cyborgs, 166 jacked command and support humans, 1,404 surveillance and attack drones, 256 UV-123 Locusts, 25 M-70C Combat Carriers, and 192 Mk-187 ACRs (Autonomous Combat Robots), it is the premier unit of the US Army's ground combat forces.

The division is the knife edge of XVIIIth ABN Corp's offensive power, and Colonel Mark Andrew Gray commands it.

The "Cherries" mill around just inside the carrier, a few steps from the troop ramp as he boards. Looking over his new headaches, the colonel is startled to see the blond woman from that annoying waking dream. For a brief moment he stares, silent. Finally aware they're awaiting orders, he points to a storage area, "Stow your gear in there, then follow me."

He waits for them to shove their duffles in the compartment. When they've finished, he strides through the inner hatch into the troop compartment and through it, into the command center, his new headaches in tow. Attached to the forward bulkhead of the command center is a large monitor, four meters wide and three high, flanked by several smaller ones. Three rows of workstations face it, seven workstations per row, twenty of which are already occupied by the Colonel's subordinate officers. On a raised platform overlooking the workspace is the commander's station.

Colonel Gray leads the "cherries" to the vacant terminal. He points to it, saying, "You'll jack in here. You will be able to "hear" everything, but not "say" anything. You do not have the sense or the smarts to direct W.I.D.G.E.T.S., and probably never will."

One of his new headaches raises her hand. It's the perplexing young blond woman, the tiniest, least impressive of the third lieutenants. She seems totally out of place, but his intuition is setting off heavy alarms, irritating him further. The colonel glares, fairly shouting, "What?"

Staring down at the deck, she mumbles something.

"*What!?*" He bellows.

Eyes round and frightened, she almost whimpers, "What's a widget?"

"My God! Not *a* widget—W.I.D.G.E.T.S.! Wholly Integrated Directable General Engagement Tactical Systems," Colonel Gray grumbles. He points to one of the Mk-17D units visible through the hatch to the troop compartment, saying sarcastically, "That is a W.I.D.G.E.T.S.—though it *is* just a cyborg, I'm certain it has a good deal more intelligence than all of you combined. I *know* it costs more than the bunch of you, which is why you're *not* to issue any directions to them. In other words, do not say or think anything. Just listen; you might learn something.

"You guys aren't really officers, not yet. You're just potens—potentials. For the record, out of the lot of you, at least two will be bounced out of the program in the next few days. You'll spend the rest of your lives in some civil service battalion, probably labor, to pay off the government's investment in you." He looks at the girl asking the question. "Two maybe three of you will be worth enough to upgrade into either Mk-4 or Mk-17 W.I.D.G.E.T.S. That's how you'll spend the rest of your lives." He glares at all of them. "Odds are only one of you will measure up to be one of us, to become J.A.C.K.S. What does J.A.C.K.S. stand for?" He points at a brown-haired young man.

His victim stammers out, "Uh, uh, Joint Advanced Command Knowledge System?"

"Are you asking me or telling me cadet?"

"Uh, um, answering your question, sir."

The colonel nods. *Damn, that kid looks like he's going to faint.* "Now, can any of you tell me why we're here?" continues Colonel Gray.

For several moments dead silence. Finally, a young man answers, "To help the Union of European States recover their lost territory."

Colonel Gray asks, "And why is that necessary?"

The "cherries" all fidget, mumbling incoherently. "Come on, at least one of you has to know what this is all about." Still nothing. He just shakes his head, disgusted. "How in Satan's beard could this happen to me?"

"I'm going to cover this once, so listen up. In 2064 the Russian Consortium tried to take Ukraine, Belarus, and the Baltic States. Though NATO had been defunct for ten years, the UK and the US supported the UES in halting the Russian advance. The battle lines halted just east of the UES eastern border, almost two hundred kilometers east of the UES states of Poland and Romania. A truce was signed, and US forces withdrew. Our main focus has been keeping the Chinese in check since then.

"Four months ago, large formations of Russian units were moved up to the truce line by the Russian Consortium. These organizations are made up of a new series of cyborgs, things we haven't seen in action before. The UES decided to move all its cyborg units, including police, to the front to counter the RC aggression. The problem we are addressing came into being because of that move.

"The UES states of Spain and Portugal decided to secede from the UES; they didn't like being backwater places anymore. With no cyborg military or police there to stop them, they declared their own "Brexit". The UES, the UK and the USA all believe this move was heavily influenced by the Russian Consortium and China. This is confirmed in that the "geese" and the "yards" are heavily equipped with Russian and Chinese weapons and equipment."

A different third lieutenant raises his hand. "What?" shouts Colonel Gray.

"Sir, what are the "geese" and the "yards"?"

The colonel replies sarcastically, "Geese, Portuguese, Yards, Spaniards."

"Oh." The poten looks startled.

Frustrated, he shakes his head. "Because the UES and UK had to keep their Cyborgs facing the RC Cyborgs, they asked us to re-establish their control of the rogue states. Hence operation Iberian

Cyclone. The goal is to secure all the lost territory from the Atlantic to the Pyrenees."

Colonel Gray pauses, waiting. There's no reaction. Nothing but blank faces. *Maybe I'm bouncing* all *these clowns.* "Our initial move was for our assault force to overrun Portugal and the western region of Spain. Almost all Portuguese forces have been destroyed, the surviving few are intermingled with Spanish units. Civil Action units are drafting "geese" for upgrade to Mk-2LE Law Enforcement Cyborgs, and UES civil authorities have taken control of all government functions in the reclaimed territory. The American Expeditionary Force is currently holding a line from Asturias in the north to Malaga in the south. XVIIIth ABN Corp's sector is from Merida to Malaga. Our sector is Merida in the north to Córdoba in the south."

He looks over the new third lieutenants. *Yep, deer in the headlights.* Colonel Gray points to the map on the large monitor, saying, "For us the next phase of the operation is to drive East to the line Guadalajara in the north and Cuenca in the south. That must be accomplished in five days or less. Any questions?"

They stare at him, looking lost. He shakes his head again. "Okay, just jack in and keep quiet." The colonel hands out jack cables. The "cherries" all jack into the network. One by one, their eyes go blank, merging with the system, their virtual sight accessing a giant 3D topographic map, its varying icons glowing a light blue. Other icons, less immediate, shimmer a fiery red-orange.

The colonel goes to his own workstation, sitting to jack in. He links to his subordinate commanders, integrating with the Corp Commander and signaling the division is standing by. Lastly, he connects to the new crop of cadets, immediately noting the little blond third lieutenant has unexpectedly high signal strength.

When jacking was first developed, it was thought that a commander could directly control all elements under his command. Then reality stepped in. Even with the drugs, neuro-pathway construction and overclocked chip implants, a single human mind could not handle the M to the Nth power of complex decisions required for hundreds, sometimes thousands, of individual units. The commanders simply burned out from the strain.

They tried augmenting the commanders with Super AI implants, they even integrated the commanders with A.S.I.N.M. It helped, but it didn't solve the problem.

Another lesson learned: it actually took longer for a single commander to direct the units than an integrated team. The military dependence on the chain of command had finally become obsolete, they claimed, until proven more vital than ever during the process.

This led to J.A.C.K.S. being developed. Riding dedicated bandwidth on A.S.I.N.M. (Artificial Super Intelligence Network Manager), J.A.C.K.S., the Joint Advanced Command Knowledge System, gives the commanders and their subordinates all the military ever wanted. Everything is done at the speed of thought. No more writing or verbalizing orders to be misinterpreted The commander thinks it, and all his jacked-in subordinates "see" his exact thoughts. The division commander provides the vision, the regimental commanders deploy their units, the battalion commanders fight their units. They are all J.A.C.K.S., all integrated in thought and action.

Further, a commander can "see" what his subordinates are aware of, down to the individual cyborg or robot. No more miscommunication in the heat of battle.

The problem is the best candidates for J.A.C.K.S. are people that border on being psychopaths. All good J.A.C.K.S. have these traits in common, lack of empathy, guilt or remorse, and shallow experiences of feelings and emotions—except anger. However, the top selections require powerful impulse control– which is required for fighting to win–and strong intuition, critical in reading an enemy commander's plans from his actions. To help keep the negative traits in check, strong neuropathways are built to direct the officer's thoughts in the "right" direction, with the deeply implanted mantra, *We exist to serve.* Therein, on shaky foundations, rests politicians' beliefs in their maintaining control of the military.

Additionally, J.A.C.K.S. aren't allowed to dream freely. It was found that unsupervised dreams caused "undesirable inefficiencies", so the rejuvenation modules, called "coffins" by their users, were developed. Once every five to nine days a J.A.C.K.S. spends ten hours in a mental recalibration "coffin".

The company commanders are all J.A.C.K.S. washouts. To payback their education costs, they are altered into cyborgs, currently either Mk-17Ds or Mk-4Hs, designed and assembled to lead the fight. The only sargeants in this army are platoon leaders, selected from the most extraordinary Mk-17Ds. Their job is to direct the squads.

In this army, there are no soldiers, only J.A.C.K.S. and W.I.D.G.E.T.S.— jacked humans and cyborgs. As far as the J.A.C.K.S. are concerned, they are the only humans in the US Army. In fact, they believe they are the only real humans, period. Everything else is either W.I.D.G.E.T.S. or potens, or politicians to whom all must pay no more than lip service.

The chronometer appears on the monitor and in their minds, showing two hours until "kickoff". First Colonel Gray reviews the Corp's current intel updates. *Nothing unexpected.* He starts pushing virtual commands for the subordinate commanders to activate, alerting their units. The "cherries" are looped into the whole process to observe it in real time.

Already in their advance positions, the recon and intel drones "wake up". The ID-34 IRD is a covert information gathering autonomous system, looking much like an old Earth grasshopper at first glance. They blanket the forward battle space, using LIDAR, thermal imaging and night vision sensors to detect targets. They also have listening capability; there is impressive documentation of these "bugs" listening to enemy commanders making plans from over a kilometer away—thereby giving the Americans a significant edge.

For the next hour, the AI systems on the carriers process the data flowing to them from the "bugs". Nearly every "yard" position is plotted, and critical targets identified. Colonel Gray shares the intelligence both with his superior and the subordinate commanders. Operational plans are modified, indirect fire target tables updated and prioritized.

Using this intel, each of the carriers' indirect fire systems, both cannon and rocket, are assigned targets, as are the locusts. The UV-123s will fill the air support roll in the opening phases of the operation. The assault drones are given their targets; the Mk-17Ds rev up for battle.

The colonel monitors message traffic, smiling proudly at the efficiency of his units. *They are magnificent.* The fly in the ointment is the confusion coming from his "cherries" in roiling, greasy waves.

As the sun sets, the elements of the 82nd ABN Div Cyborg shift to their jump-off positions. At the end of Operation Desert Storm in February 1991, the American soldiers chanted "We own the night!" This is now true. In the last two decades, the U.S. military has not launched a single daytime offensive. The advanced technology built into the American drones, equipment, W.I.D.G.E.T.S. and J.A.C.K.S. has defined its superior advantage over all comers.

With thirty minutes to zero, the combat drones take to the air. The MQ-83 Black Talon is one of the most lethal elements available to Colonel Gray, flying swiftly towards the enemy's rear formation.

At five minutes to zero the carriers' cannons unleash a storm of fire, rocket batteries launching deadly payloads into the cacophony. The colonel scowls at his "cherry" third louies; though their brains are virtually locked with the division's AI systems, they still jump at the report of cannon fire.

Smart warheads seek their assigned targets as the clock strikes zero. The assault forces move out, Colonel Gray masterfully directing the destruction. He moves his division forward with three regiments on-line, holding the fourth regiment and the ACRs in reserve. These, the exploitation forces, will be released at the exact opportune moment.

Massive amounts of data pour into the carrier's AI systems, each element reporting the results of its strikes or initial contact. The systems process the information at lightning speed, then route the results to the appropriate level of command. Though not really necessary, everything is presented on the monitors attached to the forward bulkhead of the command center.

Smart warheads find their designated targets and detonate. Locusts and drones rain auto-cannon fire down upon enemy fixed positions. In built up areas, ¾ kiloton enhanced radiation warheads explode, showering those targets with intense neutron radiation, killing man and animal alike, but leaving the structures intact for future use. Where the enhanced radiation weapons would cause too much damage or be ineffective, advanced binary nerve agents are employed. The gas is heavy, seeping down into bunkers, foxholes, and cellars, killing all it encounters. It is an orchestra of death on an unimaginable scale, and Colonel Mark Andrew Gray is the conductor.

Part of the colonel's brain monitors the reactions of the new third lieutenants. A virtual screen displays each one's face, scholastic record, service record, EEG and EKG. Empathy and Psi scores are highlighted and monitored; the Advanced AI interface analyzes the subject's very thoughts. Among J.A.C.K.S. there can be no secrets.

So far, the colonel is disappointed with them all. The only one that shows any possible usefulness is the petite blond—and what's showing is definitely *not* military potential. She would be more useful in the courtesan element of a comfort unit. Still, something lurks in an obscuring dark fog in the cherry's mind. He tries to penetrate the obscured area, but cannot match the increasing resistance. The more he tries, the more futile are his efforts. Soon, what was great discomfort blooms into real pain.

The carriers make their first jump, skimming hills and treetops to land at preselected locations. As the battle line moves forward, the carriers containing the reserves and support along with command and control move forward with them.

Not expecting the jump, all the "cherries" panic, monitors spiking. Colonel Gray shakes his head yet again, too disgusted for words.

The lead elements of the division all report enemy contact. By the end of the first hour, the 325th, 326th, and 328th Parachute Infantry Regiments Cyborg are heavily engaged. The Spanish are well armed with the latest weaponry. They have a lot of heart; unfortunately for them, that's all they have.

There hasn't been a Spanish Army since 2033, the year the member countries of the European Union all joined the Union of European States. Much like the states of the United States of America, they handed most of their sovereignty to their new overlords. The existing military and law enforcement agencies of those states were disbanded and replaced by the UES Army and police agencies. NATO's charter was repudiated and replaced by new treaties with the USA and UK.

When Spain and Portugal seceded, they rapidly formed new armies. They had to rely on men who had been in uniform forty to fifty years ago to organize and train this infant force. Because of it, they were only able to create a low-quality militia. Though it's quite large and well-armed, their tactics and skills are oriented to resist the kind of military existing four decades ago. They are no match for a modern cyborg equipped army, though they are determined to resist to the last.

Cyborgs leap into Spanish strongholds. "Yards" assault en mass, sometimes shooting their comrades in the process. The cyborg's Armadillo Armor is tough; only the most powerful "yard" weapons can penetrate it. Each Mk-17D has six CD-31C combat drones linked to it, fighting as a single entity. It's a slaughter: the cyborgs are merciless. Nearly three hundred "yards" are killed or maimed for every Mk-17 damaged or destroyed.

Not all human traits have been removed from the cyborgs. They still feel pain, still scream when they've been injured or are dying. His new third lieutenants feel the shout from every one of the dead or dying in their minds, their empathy and psi markers spike wildy. It's clear to Colonel Gray that only one of these candidates may make the cut. One cannot feel the pain of the dead and dying W.I.D.G.E.T.S. and do the job of a J.A.C.K.S.

The colonel allows the slice of his mind reserved for evaluating new third louies to do an in-depth analysis of how they are responding, while the rest of his mind directs the battle. Their responses show the group to be sub-par for J.A.C.K.S., yet two of the candidates show some interesting activity.

Most interesting is the petite blond. He looks deeper into her record. Cassandra Lynn Anderson. Twenty years old. Five-foot one inch, one hundred and four pounds, blond hair and blue eyes. Psych says she's a people pleaser, likes to help others. Loves animals, had a pet dog and a canary before entering the program. High intelligence, strong psi characteristics. An intuition score well above the superior rating. *That must be why they kept her in the program. Empathy score is way too high; she doesn't belong here.* Interestingly, he still can't penetrate the befogged portion of her mind.

The other interesting cherry is Robert Michael Hayes, twenty years old. Five-foot nine inches, one hundred and sixty-five pounds. Brown hair and brown eyes. Not very popular, no pets and few friends. Above average intelligence, solid math and spatial relationship scores. Above average psi characteristics, high aggression score. *Low empathy score, that's good. He might make a decent W.I.D.G.E.T.S., maybe even a pilot. I need to keep an eye on him.*

Unless there's a major change over the next couple of days the rest aren't worth wasting time on. Why the hell did they send these people to me? Who is doing the screening and recruiting for the academy these days?

The battle rages on. Soon the carriers are near the front lines, the sounds of battle can be heard through their armored hulls. Shortly after 02:00, the Spanish defense collapses, "yard" units retreat in disarray. Though Spanish unit commanders keep attempting to rally their troops, they are not able to reestablish a viable defense. Their situation continues to deteriorate, and by 05:00 it has degenerated into a full-fledged rout.

Colonel Gray directs his reserve regiment, the 327th Parachute Infantry Regiment Cyborg, to seize objectives deep in the enemy's rear areas, including Guadalajara and Cuenca. A third of the UV-123s move to the LZ to pick up the W.I.D.G.E.T.S. and carry them to their objectives. The regiments five M-70C Combat Carriers join the Locusts in the move to provide support to their respective battalions. By 07:00 they are flying at nap of the earth, racing forward to assigned objectives.

The colonel releases his Mk-187 ACRs along four routes of advance, an armored punch. The autonomous robots destroy everything encountered, driving hard to link up with the W.I.D.G.E.T.S. of the 327th. Anyone not equipped with an acknowledged Identification Friend or Foe (IFF) system is immediately dispatched.

Next, Colonel Gray issues directive 17 to the lead elements of his division. The battalion commanders relay it to all of their W.I.D.G.E.T.S. Directive 17 releases the Mk-17s to destroy all resistance they encounter and move to their final objectives, operating on their own initiative. Other than monitoring, the division command elements will only take back control if there is strong enemy resistance the W.I.D.G.E.T.S. cannot overcome on their own.

The colonel feels comfortable that for the next few minutes he can leave the monitoring of operations in the hands of his subordinates. He has the carrier pilot move to the location where the heaviest engagement took place, allowing him to conduct another test of his third louies, one he doesn't always get to do. He calls it the "shock" test.

Colonel Gray directs the Mk-4Hs "flying" his carrier to land with the carrier's troop ramp directly facing the most bodies visible. Once on the ground he gathers the "cherries", leading them to the troop ramp. Toggling the switch, he lowers the ramp, leading them out of the carrier. The stench of death and burnt cordite overwhelms them, like walking into a brick wall. Except for the colonel, they all drop to their hands and knees before reaching the end of the ramp.

Watching them retch their stomachs out, the colonel berates them. "You people are a disgrace. What are you doing in this program?"

When she gets control of herself, Third Lieutenant Anderson shouts, "They took me from my family against my will; I never wanted to be here!"

The colonel walks back to her. He kneels down to lift her head, looking into her eyes. For a moment he considers what to say. "The government can take anyone if that taking meets military necessity, even you. What confuses me is how any of you, and you in particular, wound up here. Your intuition score and academics are what the J.A.C.K.S. program is looking for, but your empathy and psi scores rule you out for anything except courtesan work. Yet here you are." He looks over at the others. "You do have minimal characteristic and scholastic scores barely qualifying you for the program. It makes no sense that they sent any of you to me." He looks back at the petite blond, "But you, there's absolutely no reason for you to be here."

He slowly stands, helping the young woman up as he does. "Back inside, now." The colonel watches them scramble to get back inside. He follows them in, raising the ramp. Striding back to his station, he continues to wonder about Third Lieutenant Anderson. There is something about her he's not comprehending.

For the next seventy hours the combat continues, Colonel Gray keeping the division rolling forward, linking up with his deep penetration units along the way. As they advance, the W.I.D.G.E.T.S. of the 82nd ABN Div Cyborg encounter pockets of stiff resistance. Had they been men instead of cyborgs, they might have called the "yard" defenders heroic.

Many times, officers chose to rally their troops by jumping on a vehicle or bunker, waving the flag of the Kingdom of Spain. Their soldiers dig in their heels, fighting and dying around these tattered banners, fierce souls giving the last full measure for a lost cause.

Many of these courageous warriors strap explosives to themselves, attempting to swarm any Mk-17 encountered. Dozens are slaughtered, all hoping that one will hug a W.I.D.G.E.T.S. to detonate himself or herself, taking down the apparently soulless monsters. Some succeed.

At the forty-five hours mark, the system alerts him of a potential problem among the "cherries". Colonel Gray checks their readouts. All but two are peaking at emotional overload, empathy and psi scores are approaching the danger level. *They are feeling too much!*

Lieutenant Hayes is solid, only his aggression score is peaking. Further, his empathy and psi levels are extremely low. Colonel Gray likes what he's seeing there, smiling. *Wow, decades ago they would have described Lieutenant Hayes as a psychopath, just like they said about me when I was a third lieutenant. He might make a J.A.C.K.S. after all.*

Cassandra Anderson is opposite. Her aggression score is near zero, empathy and psi scores are above the redline, her heart rate exceeding one hundred twenty-six. *She might burst!*

The colonel commands, "Lieutenants, unjack." All of them except the petite blond disconnect from the system. "Unjack now, lieutenant Anderson!"

"No, sir!"

"UNJACK NOW!"

"No! Someone has to be here! Someone has to hear them! Someone has to know they lived!"

"UNJACK LIEUTENANT!"

"NO! These people are dying; someone has to care!"

"They are not people, they are not human, they are just W.I.D.G.E.T.S. UNJACK!"

"NO!"

At that moment, two Mk-17s are destroyed by explosions. For a brief instant their minds shout out in pain. The release of fear and hurt hits the petite blond like a tidal wave. For a fraction of a second she feels she is drowning in an ocean of emotion, a tidal wave of psychic energy. Her readouts all spike. Then it's over, the intense pain and terror gone. Her mind crashes; she falls, limp, to the deck.

At first the colonel thinks, *I should just leave her there.* His next thought is, *She disobeyed me, I should shoot her.* His third thought is, *Damn.* "Medtech," is all he says.

A Mk-4H Medtech enters the command center, carrying the young third lieutenant into the med compartment.

By hour eighty-four, the division has achieved all its objectives, only the mopping up is left to do. Colonel Gray smiles to himself, *The 82nd ABN Div Cyborg is the best division in the US Army.* As the division adjusts its lines, finishing the mop up to the south of it, its brother unit, the 101st ABN Div Cyborg, completes its advance. XVIIIth ABN Corp's third unit, the 3rd ACR, screens to the north as the US Vth Corp catches up. XVIIIth ABN Corp's Commander, Brigadier General Barnes, is quite pleased; he beat all the Corps to his objectives.

The command carrier sets up next to one of the last battles for this phase of the operation. The colonel looks over the devastation, filled with satisfaction. Even the inevitable terrible sights of the battle's finale don't bother him. *This mess will be cleaned up when the army's salvage and incineration unit arrives, until then, this is what victory looks like.*

As he stands at the base of the troop ramp, he hears footsteps, turning to see Third Lieutenant Anderson stride down the ramp behind him. This is the first time he's seen her outside the med compartment since she "crashed". As she reaches the end of the ramp, the colonel steps aside. She steps onto the ground to stop beside Colonel Gray.

They stand side-by-side for several moments in strained silence. After a while, Cassandra asks, "Now what?" Before the colonel can answer, she notices something moving among some bodies. Third Lieutenant Anderson steps haltingly toward it, Colonel Gray following.

A severely wounded Mk-17 is among half a dozen dead "yards". Cassandra kneels down beside it. The cyborg is missing its right leg, and the right forearm is shattered, its left leg is destroyed from just below the knee. Sparks rain from all the damaged parts, a fiery nimbus. The Mk-17s' Armadillo Protection System is penetrated in numerous spots, the helmet split open to reveal the cyborg's face, blood dripping from its mouth. The markings on its Armadillo Battle Skin designate it as a Sargent.

"We have to help him," she says.

"It's just a W.I.D.G.E.T.S., it's too damaged to save. The salvage unit will be along shortly to recover what can be reused," replies the colonel.

"You're just going to kill him?"

"It's not a him, it's an it."

She reaches out to smooth a hand over the Sargent's face. "You're wrong, he is a person, a real person." At her touch, something unexpected happens. The petite blond's hands start to glow a pale blue, her eyes light up. The cyborg locks vision with her. They stay connected for several moments, before the Mk-17 breathes its last, slumping against her. Gently easing the remains down, she stands up, eyes still aglow. It fades slowly, too slowly to mistake it not being real.

Standing there in shock, the colonel tries to call three W.I.D.G.E.T.S. to help, but all his communication to his units is jammed. *This can't be! I'm always in direct mental contact with my commands! What is she?* He tries to force his commands through the block, to no avail; he has never heard of something like this, let alone seen it.

Cassie turns to look deep into his eyes—he feels he's falling into a deep, dark hole. For the first time since he was upgraded to J.A.C.K.S., he's afraid. Down and down he falls, then suddenly he's back standing beside Third Lieutenant Anderson trying to remember why they have come out onto the field. The last thing he recalls is standing at the base of the ramp.

"You haven't answered my question, Colonel. Now what?" Cassie asks

"Well, Miss Anderson, you're no longer a third lieutenant. My recommendation will be that they place you in the courtesan element of a comfort unit instead of a labor battalion. Perhaps they'll follow my recommendation. I think Third Lieutenant Hayes might become a J.A.C.K.S.; if not he will be upgraded as a W.I.D.G.E.T.S. The rest of your classmates will go into a labor battalion. All of you will be leaving for your reviews, evaluations, and new assignments in an hour."

"Thank you. I never wanted any part of this."

"That doesn't matter. We exist to serve."

"That's what they teach us." She looks him in the eye, facing him directly, taking his big right hand in her smaller left. A tingle like a mild electric shock emanates from her touch. With her free hand she touches his left temple lightly. Another tingle. "Goodbye, Colonel. I truly feel sorry for you." Dropping his hand, she walks back up the ramp.

He watches her for a long moment. Before she enters the carrier, he calls out, "Miss Anderson, wait a moment." She stops, turning to face him again. From an arm's length away, the colonel asks incredulously, "Why do you feel sorry for me?"

Her lips set in a grim line, she replies, "I feel sorry for you because you think you are human, but you lack all that makes someone human."

"What do you mean by that?" He growls.

"Like that, you're always angry, always ready to fight, to tear into someone, verbally or physically."

"That's how I'm supposed to be," he barks back.

"Yes, it is. And you don't feel. You send soldiers out to die, not caring about them as people, only that they do their jobs."

"That's my job. That's what we do—we serve, we sacrifice. That's what makes us human, better than all of you."

"No, that's what makes you less than human. You're more of an *it* than the W.I.D.G.E.T.S. You don't care about anyone, only the mission. Just winning the battle. No one means anything to you, and you mean nothing to anyone else. That is so sad, that's why I feel sorry for you."

"Goodbye, Miss Anderson," he growls, pushing past her.

"Colonel."

He stops, turning again to face the tiny woman. "I saw inside your mind, just like you saw inside mine. They took so much away from you when they upgraded you. They took away what really matters. The worst is they took away your ability to truly dream. But it's right there, Colonel, just below the surface. And it just might get out—it just might come back."

He stomps off up the ramp.

At 14:30 the UV-123 lifts off, taking Colonel Gray's headaches away.

The "cherries" are gone, the battle is winding down, and everything is quiet. Colonel Gray has sent in his replacement request. The division's losses were light, but it will still take two days to replace them all. It seems like a good time to rejuvenate.

Colonel Gray goes into the rejuvenation chamber to enter his coffin. The lid closes; the system is activated. He closes his eyes, shutting down. Then something happens that hasn't happened since Mark Andrew Gray was upgraded to a J.A.C.K.S.

He dreams.

She Decided to Be a Vampire

By Erika M Szabo

Every kid in town knew that old Mrs. Robbins was a vampire. Their parents laughed at their childish fantasies, but the kids had evidence as a result of spying on the old woman for months. Mrs. Robbins always wore black clothes and never left the house. At least never during the daytime, until...

The most compelling piece of evidence was when Billy Atkins said that he saw her watching the sunrise on her porch one morning, and when the sun was about to come up, she clasped her chest and ran inside. "You see what I'm talking about? Vampires burn to ashes when the sunlight hits them."

It hadn't been so bad at first, having a vampire in the neighborhood. Moreover, it was exciting. They knew she couldn't harm them in the daytime, and they'd be locked in their houses safely at night. "Everybody knows that a vampire can't come into your house unless you invite them in," Billy assured his still apprehensive friends.

But then, even Billy started to feel a little uneasy when they noticed that Mrs. Robbins began to venture out of the house more often. She'd only go out after sunset, and she'd only go as far as the front lawn and a few days later up to the gate. She did the same thing every evening. She'd stand there holding onto the closed gate, staring at the street. Then slowly she'd reach into her pocket and pull out her keys, rattling them with a back-and-forth motion of her wrist.

The kids saw her more and more at night and later in the early morning too. She'd stay until the sun came up, and then she'd clutch her chest and run inside. This went on for a few weeks and the boys were getting bored when taking their turns to watch the *vampire's* movements. But then one night Scott, the lanky teenager who was watching her from behind the azalea bush in his garden gasped and jumped when the old woman slowly opened the gate and took a shaky step onto the sidewalk.

A few days later she started getting closer to the street.

Every night she'd rattle the keys harder until the neighbor's dog began to bark at her. But old Mrs. Robbins didn't pay the dogs any mind. She just stood there rattling her keys. That's when Billy Atkins came up with a plan. "Our parents don't believe us, so we must do something before this bloodsucker would suck us dry!" he shouted. "Let's sneak into her house at night and take a picture of her coffin. Then they'd believe us," he said to his best friend, Johnny Miller.

"No way!" Johnny shrunk back. "I ain't going in there!"

"And why would she have a coffin?" Bobby, Billy's scrawny brother asked.

"All vampires sleep in a coffin, dummy. Everybody knows that!" Billy snarled at his brother. "Besides, if we can get a picture of it, then our parents will have to believe us."

Nobody in their six-member gang volunteered to join Bobby, so they drew straws to see who would be the one to sneak into Mrs. Robbins' house with him while she was out rattling her keys. David, their chubby, blond friend drew the shortest one to everyone else's relief. David wasn't happy, as a matter of fact, he was scared out of his mind. But his fear of being teased for the rest of his life as being a coward painted a dreary picture in his mind, so he remained quiet.

The next night, while Mrs. Robbins was standing by her gate, David and Bobby snuck into the house through the front door. It wasn't hard; Mrs. Robbins left the door wide open.

As they stepped over the threshold, they noticed that the house had an oppressive feel to it. It was stiflingly hot and smelled like mothballs. David clutched his phone tightly in his sweaty hand as he scanned the living room for the coffin. There was no sign of it.

"I guessed there wouldn't be in here," Bobby whispered. "Let's check the bedroom."

They tiptoed down the hall on shaky legs. Bobby pushed the door to the bedroom open, and it gave out a loud creak. He whipped his head around to see if Mrs. Robbins had heard the noise, but he saw the old woman still standing by the gate, rattling her keys.

There was no coffin in the bedroom either. "Maybe it's in the basement," Bobby speculated.

"No! Please let's not go down there!" David pleaded, close to panic.

"Come on you scaredy cat!" Bobby growled heading toward the basement door. David hesitantly but followed his friend.

The door was old, and the paint was peeling off of it. Bobby felt sweat beading up on his forehead as he stared at the door. He couldn't tell if it was nerves or just the heat. He pushed the door open and switched on the flashlight on his phone, but it only lit about halfway down the staircase. He took a hesitant step down, and that's when they heard the front door closing, followed by thudding footsteps.

They couldn't run; their only chance was to go down the steps and hide. David closed the basement door behind them as quietly as he could, and they started down the steps.

But there must have been a missing step because Bobby's foot found only air, and he tumbled headlong the rest of the way down. David screamed and Bobby dropped his phone. The screen shattered, but the flashlight was still on. He jumped up and swept the beam of light around the room.

"This looks like some kind of laboratory," David whispered, staring at the shiny, metal table that was loaded with glass vials and jars.

On the shelves by the wall, they saw large glass jars. The jars were filled with light green liquid, and each one had something floating in it.

As their eyes focused, they saw what was inside the jars. A scream gathered in Bobby's throat but came out as a whimper. David's scream was loud enough, however, for Mrs. Robbins to hear him. The basement door flung open, and light poured into the room.

"Who's down here?" Mrs. Robbins called out.

Bobby frantically scanned the walls for another exit, but there was only one way out, and Mrs. Robbins was standing between them and the door. Mrs. Robbins swung her flashlight beam over them.

David dropped to his knees. "Please don't kill us!"

They heard a click, and the sharp fluorescent lights above their heads came on. Bobby dared not look to his right, where he knew the jars of the strange creatures were.

"So, you found out my secrets," Mrs. Robbins said as she watched David staring at the jars.

"Those… those almost look like babies," Bobby mumbled, looking at the old woman with fear.

"We won't tell anybody. Promise!" David cried.

You're not in any danger, silly boy," Mrs. Robbins laughed. She walked over to the jars and rested a hand on one of them. She shook her head. "These two were the children I've lost a long time ago. Neither of them made it to full term. I lost Vivienne when I was only four months pregnant with her," she caressed the jar with the tiny fetus inside. "And this is little John, he made it a month longer but wasn't viable either," the old woman sighed tears rolling down her cheeks. "You see, I'm a scientist. I dedicated my life to research genetic disorders, and when I retired, I opened my lab here."

The boys were too scared to look at the jars, they stood frozen with fear.

"Come on, boys," Mrs. Robbins said, wiping the tears off her face. "Have a cup of tea with me, and I won't tell your parents that you snuck in here." Mrs. Robbins turned and walked up the stairs without waiting for their response. After a moment's hesitation, the boys followed her.

They sat on Mrs. Robbins' old red couch as she put the kettle on, and a couple of minutes later, they were both sipping lavender tea out of delicate teacups.

Bobby noticed that Mrs. Robbins' hand shook as she lifted the cup. "Mrs. Robbins," he hesitated. "Can I ask you something?"

"Of course," the old lady nodded.

"You said those were your children."

Mrs. Robbins shifted uncomfortably in her seat. "That's right," she said.

"How come they came out like that, all twisted up and deformed?" Bobby asked, his face flushed red. "I'm sorry, I didn't mean to…" he apologized.

She stared into her teacup for a moment. "It's okay," she sighed. "That's what I've been working on all my life, to find out why some babies are born with a disease that deforms their little bodies."

"Did you find out why?" David's eyes lit up and inquired, now feeling a little less scared and more curious. "Because my mom said that she lost my sister before I was born but she didn't say why."

"There could be a lot of reasons for babies not to be able to develop normally," the old lady replied. "My babies were deformed because I was taking a particular medication for morning sickness." Her voice became hoarse and bowed her head.

"A medication that the doctor is giving you can do that?" Bobby gasped.

"Unfortunately, it can. Sometimes, we notice the bad side effects years later, after hundreds of people had been using them."

"Mrs. Robbins, I'm sorry it happened to you," David said.

"Thank you, son," the old lady whispered. "It was a long time ago, but still hurts inside. I was too afraid to try to have more babies. I wish I did…"

"It must be very lonely to live alone," Bobby said.

"Well, my husband left me a long time ago, and my only sister lives far away."

"Why don't you go out and make friends?" he asked.

Mrs. Robbins took a sharp breath. "Do you know what agoraphobia is?"

Bobby shook his head.

"It means I'm too scared to leave the house,' she said. "Too much open space, too much noise, and too many people are suffocating me, and I panic. I can make it as far as the lawn some nights, but then the daylight comes, and the world opens up, and I've got to run back inside.

"But you've been going outside every night," he said. "I've seen you."

"I'm trying," she replied. She stared into her tea with a troubled look on her face. "My sister is dying," she said. "They say she's got a few months left, but it's my last chance to see her before she dies. I'm trying to overcome my fear, but I'm afraid it's too late."

"Why do you rattle your keys?"

"They're my car keys," she said. "And anything I hold these days rattles because my fingers shake," she gave out a short, bitter laugh. "But I'm fooling myself," she went on. "I haven't driven that car in over ten years. Even if I could make it as far as to sit in it, I couldn't drive."

"And we thought you were a vampire," David said.

Mrs. Robbins snorted in her tea. "A vampire?" she asked, hardly believing what the young boy said.

"Well, you only ever come out in its dark and run back to the house when the sun comes up, and Billy said that meant you were a vampire."

To his surprise, Mrs. Robbins began to laugh. "I suppose that makes more sense than to understand why someone is afraid of the outside," she said.

"Yes, it does," David replied. "Everybody heard of vampires, but I don't think anybody knows what agoraphobia is."

"Agoraphobia," Mrs. Robbins said, a soft smile lighting her face. "It's a disease that cripples a lot of people."

"But Mrs. Robbins, how can anybody be afraid of the outside?" Bobby asked.

Mrs. Robbins' lips creased into a frown. "Well, if there's one thing I've learned in life, it's that living in fear is like standing under an avalanche. If you don't move out of the way, the snow just keeps piling up on you, higher and higher, and eventually, you get so deep that you can never dig your way out."

"It's a shame you're not a vampire," David said.

"Why is that?"

"Because if you were a vampire, you wouldn't have to be afraid and you could drive your car all night or even in daytime. I don't think there's anything on the outside tougher than a vampire. Billy says that vampires can't go out in the sunlight, but he figured that they could just wear sunblock."

Mrs. Robbins smiled. "Yes," she said. "I suppose they could."

The boys went home, but that wasn't the last time they had tea at Mrs. Robbins' place. Once they knew she wasn't a vampire, David and the other kids started to stop by. She would make them lavender tea with honey and baked cookies, and to this day, the boys never had anything that tasted so good. The boys helped her to clean the house, mow the lawn, and do her shopping. In return, she taught them everything she knew about science.

The very last time David and Bobby went to Mrs. Robbins' house, she wasn't there. Instead, there was a note on the door that simply read, *Last night I decided to be a vampire.* Her car was gone, and a week later Bobby received a letter from her.

Dear boys!

Thanks to you boys, I gained enough courage to start my car. And then I was thinking of what you said, I didn't panic, and I started driving. At first, I only drove at night, but then I bought sunscreen, and I didn't panic driving in the daytime either. Thanks to you, I can be with my sister in her final days in California.

With much love, Gladys Robbins

The boys kept in touch with Mrs. Robbins for a few years until they received a letter from her niece that she passed away in her sleep.

Although they only knew her for a short time, they've never forgotten her. Every time they were too afraid to do something that they really wanted to do, they remembered Mrs. Robbins and how she decided to be a vampire.

T'is Was the Night

By Alan Zacher

It was two days before Christmas, and in the small town of Louisiana, Missouri, snow had blanketed the land—making the very air itself feel more Christmasy.

The town of Louisiana, Missouri, is a lazy, old, town, with an aging population of just under two thousand people, most of whom are of German descent. The town is in Pike County, and it's a river town along the banks of the mighty Mississippi River. It's in the northeast part of the state and is about 150 miles from St. Louis and is just south of the town of Hannibal, which the town people of Louisiana have a vile dislike of—well, those people in Hannibal are so "uppity", what with the town's fame of Mark Twain and such.

A hundred-and-two people live in town, and ninety-seven percent of the population are farmers and live on their small farms. These are hard-working, good, people. Ninety-nine percent of them are strict Baptists—and are even stricter Republicans. But, like I said, they're good, giving, people. You would like them—but then, there is the other three percent of the population. These are the "hill" folks of Pike County. They live in wooden shacks—well, the more "uppity" ones of them do—in the thick woods and hills that lie far distance from the town and farms.

These "hill" people are a rowdy bunch—at best. They live by their own rules and have next to nothing to do with the town's people. Ninety-nine percent of them can barely read or write, and they only marry their kind. In general, they want no dealings with the "outside" world—most particularly with, in this order: Revenuers; police; government, both federal and state; doctors; lawyers; Insurance salesmen, and on and on. Most of them are religious, though. On the first Saturday evening of the month, they gather in the room-size tent of Reverend Howard Davis of The First Church of God, and you can hear them all whooping and hollering and dancing in place and praising the resurrected King of Kings, while the Reverend Davis works himself up into such a teasy—filled with the Holy Spirit—that he passes out, crushing to death the two snakes held in hand. All of these "hill" people are dirt poor, eking out a living—when they get the gumption to work, that is—selling chopped-down trees, selling the skinned coats of animals, and making and selling moonshine whiskey.

No, the town's people—and the farmers—want next-to-nothing to do with these "hill" people—and vice-versa—but there is one thing that they all agree on and cherish: In the existence of Mo-Mo, aka, The Missouri Monster. An eight-to-ten-foot-tall, hairy, ape-like creature.

Sure, of course, it's a Bigfoot—but don't EVER say this to anyone from Louisiana, Missouri—you will most definitely walk away with fewer teeth.

Mo-Mo is special. He ain't no dang run-of-the-mill Bigfoot—he's their—the town of Louisiana's—Bigfoot! Why, he's been around Pike County since the time of Moses—and many have seen him, too—and very few have even had an "encounter" with him, or, at least, that's what the town's newspaper always calls it; an "encounter". Take Mrs. Schultz, for example. Ten years ago, the town was celebrating the construction and the opening of its first high school. Well, everyone was asked to bring food. Mrs. Schultz had baked two cherry pies. She had set the first cherry pie baked on the ledge of the open kitchen window to cool. She left the kitchen, and when she had returned, the pie was gone. She had thought that her mischievous son had stolen the pie. To teach him a lesson, she sat the second cherry pie baked on top of that ledge and stood to one side of that window, out of sight, with a broom in hand, ready for action. When she heard a noise at the window, she let the bottom half of that broom fly. It had smacked Mo-Mo square in the face. When Mrs. Schultz saw him, she fainted. It had made her a celebrity of the town, though. So much so that several ladies of the town had tried to repeat Mrs. Schultz's success. But, no. It never worked again. Mrs. Mayor had tried doing it one day with a rhubarb pie, but when she returned to the kitchen, she had found the pie thrown up against the wall opposite the open window. People figured that Mo-Mo didn't like rhubarb pie.

Now meet one of these "hill" people.

Leroy Ferris has lived in the hills of Pike County all of his thirty-three years of life. He's a relatively short man, 5 ft, 6" tall—but he is built like an ox and is just as strong as one, too. He rarely ever bathes—and never in wintertime—well, Muller's Creek is just too dang cold to bathe during winter. The color of the pupils of his eyes is the same color as his shoulder-length-long, unruly, wild-looking, hair: raven black, which is also the same color as his ZZ Top-looking beard. His perpetual wear of clothing is his worn-out, dirty, bib-overhauls and a worn-out denim shirt, and his thick, leather, boots.

Leroy Ferris is by far the best maker of moonshine whiskey in all of Pike County—and this skill has made Leroy much money, which he keeps stored in large, glass, jars that are—he not trusting banks—buried deep in the ground of several of the neighboring hills, near the several, makeshift, wooden, community, shacks that he and his fellow hill-folk use to make the moonshine elixir and to hide from the sheriff and the dreaded—hated!—Revenuers.

In younger days, Leroy was quite a rabble-rouser; getting drunk with his best friend, Billy-Jo Smith, and raising cane—and if you were foolish enough to cross him, he'd just as soon stab you or shoot you than to turn his other cheek to you, like the Good Book says. Yes, in younger days, Leroy, was full of "wild-oats-to-sow"—but at the age of nineteen and "setting his cap" for sixteen-year-old Sarah-Jean Fisher—the prettiest gal in all the hills—all of Leroy's rabblerousing and "sowing-of-wild-oats" ended. He married Sarah-Jean.

It had been a "contested" marriage—meaning that six other young bucks had also "set their caps" for the love of Sarah-Jean. It was one of the "rules" of the hills that all suiters involved had to settle the matter by fighting each other in a public display of fisticuffs. Not to worry. Leroy had whipped them all.

It had been a good marriage. Leroy had loved her, and she had loved him—why, Leroy had even built her one of the finest wooden shacks on Morgan's hill. Why, it had a wood-burning stove, and the "odd-house" was a two-seater and was just a "no-smell" away from their home.

The years passed, and eleven years ago, Sarah-Jean became pregnant. Leroy was overjoyed. He had wished—hoped! Prayed!—that the child would be a boy. Sadly, it wasn't, and even sadder,--tragic!—on the night that he had helped Sarah-Jean give birth to the child, Sarah-Jean died. Just before she had died, she had made Leroy promise her that he would see to it that the child would have a better life than what they had had—that she would have schooling; would learn reading and writing; would wear dresses; would leave these hills; would-would become "citified". With a breaking heart and in tears, Leroy had kept promising her that he would—he had kept promising her that until the very moment that she had died.

Leroy had named the newborn child Bobby-Jo. He came to love her dearly, but he had raised her as if she had been born a boy—and she had grown into being one heck of a tough tomboy. Leroy was exceedingly proud of her. She was the "apple of his eye", but now, the promise that he had made so long ago to his dying woman, was haunting him.

With just one more night before Christmas Eve, in one of Leroy's wooden shacks, this one on the hill of Adelburg Hill—with the lit kerosene lamp glowing on top of an old, wooden, table, and with the makeshift, lighted, fireplace made of stone and mud against the west wall of the room, Leroy chided Bobby-Jo again.

"Youse are goin', Bobby-Jo!" Leroy yelled angrily at her again. "Youse are goin"!" he repeated. "It's all arranged. Youse are leavin' tomorrow … Like I told youse—Billy-Jo's cousin is a good woman. She's a widower with two children—two girls. She needs money. She's agreed to let youse live in her house and goin' to school … Youse a-goin'! Tomorrow!"

"But whys, Pa?!" Bobby-Jo pleaded, sitting on top of a chopped tree truck that had been turned right-side up and was positioned to the left side of the table: Bobby-Jo wearing worn-out, dirty, bib-overhauls and a denim shirt. "Whys? Don't youse want me no more?!"

"Don'ts be givin' me that hogwash!" Leroy yelled at her. "I told ya. Ya ma wanted youse to have schoolin'—readin' and writin'. She wanted youse out of these hills. She wanted youse citified. The widower Salford lives in town."

"But whys now, Pa?!" Bobby-Jo continued pleading. "Whys?!"

"Just 'cuz," he replied, sharply.

"Whys, Pa?!" she keep asking. "Whys?!"

"'cuz-'cus!" Leroy replied, waving his arms and hands at her dismissively. Then, in a fix of explosive, exasperated and frustrated, anger, Leroy shouted: "'cuz youse changin'! It be time!"

"What?!" Bobby-Jo cried, totally confused. "Changin'?! … What does youse mean, Pa?"

"Can't youse see?!" he shouted, angrily, extending his right arm out and pointing with his hand to Bobby-Jo's just beginning budding breast. "Youse becomin' a woman."

"Oh, is that all," she replied, dismissively, much relieved. "Shoot. That ain't nothin'. Why, I can still lick the tar out of any boy my size— and I can belch and fart louder than any of "em, too."

"See! See!" Leroy cried. "Youse ain't got no manners at tall … Yourn ma was right. You need citifin'. Youse need a woman's learnin'. Youse got to—"

"But, Pa!" Bobby-Jo cried, in a pleading, whining, voice. "Youse promised, Pa!" she continued, protesting. "Youse promised! … Tomorrow is Christmas Eve, and youse said that the North Star is at its brightest on that night—to guide people, like it had guided The Three Wise Men to baby Jesus. Youse said that when youse was fourteen, youse and Billy-Jo was raccoon hurtin' on that night on Morgan's Hill, and that youse got thirty, so youse told Billy-Jo that youse was goin' down to Morgan's Creek. Youse left the woods and came to Morgan's Creek, and with the brightness of the North Star — there he was as big as life!—youse saw him! Mo-Mo. He was gettin' a drink of water, and he stoods up and looks at youse and youse looks at him! Then, he walks away! … Youse saw him, Pa!—and youse promised, Pa! Youse promised that tomorrow night we'd go lookin' for Mo-Mo!"

"I knows that I did, Bobby-Jo," Leroy replied, sorrowfully, "but the wid—"

Suddenly, Leroy—and Bobby-Jo, too—heard the cowbells ring. Earlier that day, Leroy had strung a line of rope around the perimeter of the shack, tying the line to trees. He had, then, attached cowbells to the line.

"Revenuers!" Bobby-Jo cried, alarmed.

There were three firearms to the south side of the door to the shack—a Winchester Semi-Automatic rifle: a 16-gauge shotgun, and a 4-10-gauge shotgun.

Leroy moved quickly to the door, the door was made of planks of wood nailed together—grabbing the Winchester rifle as he did so. Bobby-Jo followed behind him, grabbing the 4-10 shotgun.

Standing at the door, listening, Leroy looked down to his right side and saw Bobby-Jo standing there with the 4-10 shotgun in hand.

In a hushed voice, Leroy chided her: "Puts that weapon down! Youse too young to fight!"

"But, Pa!" Bobby-Jo protested. I wanna—"

"Don't be sassin' me!" Leroy demanded. "Puts that weapon down and gets over by the fireplace and squats down!"

Reluctantly, she did.

Leroy went back to listen at the door.

A few seconds later, from just beyond the door, also in a shushed, nervous-sounding, voice, Leroy heard: "Leroy! Leroy! It's me! It's me! Billy-Jo! Let me in!"

Leroy quickly raised the makeshift latch on the door and opened the door. A tall, slender-built, bearded, man, who was wearing dirty-looking, worn-out, jeans, a clean-looking, plaid-colored, shirt, an old, leather, coat, and a hunter's cap with built-in earmuffs attached to it, came swooping inside.

"Billy-Jo!" Leroy cried, shocked at seeing Billy-Jo. "What far youse doin' in these woods tonight?!"

Billy-Jo was a good ole boy of thirty-eight years old. When he was fourteen years fourteen-years-old, he had tried to out-head-butt the family goat. The goat won, leaving Billy-Jo a bit touched in the head, but the goat was okay.

"Happy tomorrow birthday, Leroy," Billy-Jo stated, most cheerfully and heartily.

"Tomorrow ain't my birthday, Billy-Jo," Leroy replied, flatly. "Tomorrow is Christmas Eve—but what is youse doin' here?"

"I've been searchin' far youse—all night, Leroy!" Billy-Jo cried, nervously. "These hills are full of Jefferson"—the local sheriff, Jefferson Davis— "his deputies and a whole mess of ATF men."

"Who?!" Leroy replied, not knowing the term "ATF".

Billy-Jo, suddenly, looked even more nervous now.

"Oh, that's what Revenuers is called," he replied, cautiously. "— And these hills are full of 'em! … They got most of us—and they REALLY want you, Leroy!"

"What's this all 'bout. Billy-Jo?!"

"Oh, it ain't nothin' but governerment!" Billy-Jo cursed. "Ole Jefferson is up far re-a-election, and the 'uppity' sitzens of Louisiana wants moonshinin' stopped—I'm leavin'! 'fore they get me! … You-you best be gettin' out, too, Leroy—'fore they gets you!"

Leroy was deep in thought.

"What?" he replied, being shaken from his thinking. "Oh, yeah. Yeah … I got one more run to make—that-that guy from St. louie you sent me—that-that Mr. Johnston. I'm meetin' him tomorrow at four … I got the whiskey all made and jugged. All I have to do is pack it on the back of my truck. It's all at my shack at Morgan's Hill. I tolds him to meet me at the bend in Morgan's Creek. That's only ten minutes from town." Thumbing his right thumb back towards Bobby-Jo, Leroy continued: "Once I drops her off at yourns cuzen, I'll drive back to Morgan's Creek; meet-up with that Johnston; get my money; give him the whiskey and get lost 'til summer on Fisher Hill."

"Sounds good, Leroy!" Billy-Jo cried, excitedly. "They'll never finds youse on Fisher's Hill! Youse too smart far 'em, Leroy! Yes, sir! …Well, I best be goin'."

Leroy open the door for him.

Before Billy-Jo left, he said to Leroy: "Happy tomorrow birthday, Leroy … Youse-youse been a good friend."

The next morning, Leroy packed up his three weapons, the rifle and the two shotguns—leaning them up against the tattered front seat of the cab of his old pick-up truck. He and Bobby-Jo, then, left for Morgan's Hill.

It had taken Leroy about an hour to drive to his wooden shack on Morgan's Hill. Once there, he loaded up the jugs of whiskey into the bed of his truck. Then, he did something that he had just hated to do— but he had thought that he had better do it: With an ax, he busted up his still. It was about ten am, and he had a few hours to kill before he had to drop off Bobby-Jo at Billy-Jo's cousin and had to meet Mr. Johnston. There was much tension between him and Bobby-Jo—she wasn't speaking to him. Knowing how much she liked hunting; Leroy asked her if she wanted to go possum hunting.

"I guess," she replied, flatly.

Leroy knew that they wouldn't see any possums, but, at least, it would take their minds off of what they were both dreading.

They trampled in the woods for about two hours, when Leroy, sitting down on a long, fallen, log, stated: "Let's rest a-spell."

Bobby-Jo sat down beside him.

From the right pocket of the heavy coat that he was wearing, the coat made from cow skin that elderly Mary-lee Shepard, a kin of Leroy's, had made for him, and one for Bobby-Jo, too—Leroy removed two chunks of dried, smoked, beef. He handed one of them to Bobby-Jo.

As they ate, Leroy—fed up with Bobby-Jo's silence—stated, with exasperated impatience: "Youse know, this ain't no punishment. I'm doin' this far yourns own good … Tries to understands, Bobby-

Jo … I've lived in these here hills all of my life—and I know nonthin'! … I'm an igornant, nothin', hillbilly—why, there's a whole world beyond these hills that I don't know of … Ya ma didn't wants that far youse—and neither does I!"

Bobby-Jo remained silent.

"Okay, thens," Leroy stated, adamantly. "I'lls made a deal with youse … Youse live with the Widdor and youse goes to that school 'til summer, and if youse still don'ts like it, I'll comes and gets youse."

"Youse will?!" Bobby-Jo cried, ecstatically.

"Yes," he replied, and stuck out his right hand to her. "Deal?"

To seal the "deal", she first spit on her right hand and, then, she started to raise her hand to Leroy's waiting hand.

"Youse see?!" he chided her. "Youse see?! … Now, spittin' in youns hand is just uncitified!"

At three-thirty pm, Leroy was driving out of the woods of Morgan's hills and had just turned onto the one-lane of concrete pavement of the road that led to the town of Louisiana. Bobby-Jo was seated next to him, only the three weapons leaning up against the front seat of the cab of the pick-up truck separated them.

Within a half hour, it would be dark.

To Leroy's right side was Morgan's Creek. It ran parallel to the road.

He passed the bend in the creek. Leroy knew that that bend in the creek meant that the town of Louisiana was only ten miles away.

Dang! Leroy cursed, silently, at the thought of this all happening so fast. *Dang!* He repeated, silently—but then, he shouted: "What in tar-nation is!"

About thirty yards ahead of him, blocking the road—were three sheriff patrol vehicles and one plain, silver, Ford Taurus. Standing crouched behind the vehicles—with rifles in their hands—were Jefferson Davis, the local sheriff—three of his deputies and a man dressed in a dark-colored, expensive-looking, suit, a matching-colored tie, a white dress shirt, an expensive-looking, uppity, black hat and a dark-colored topcoat. Leroy immediately recognized that man to be Mr. Johnston from St. Louis who was going to buy Leroy's moonshine whiskey.

Leroy slammed on the brakes of his old pick-up truck.

Quickly and panicking, Leroy shot a look into the rearview mirror of his truck. As with in the road ahead of him, there were also three more sheriff patrol vehicles behind him—these vehicles were also about thirty yards away, and they were also parked and blocking the road, with three more of Sheriff Davis's deputies crouching behind the vehicles with rifles in hand.

"Dang!" Leroy cried, angrily. "I been set-up! … Billy-Jo set me up!"

Leroy looked to his right. There, by the bank of the creek, were four, long, fallen, trees—all of them bunched up together. Leroy, then, looked to his left—looking at the woods. Yes, the woods! The woods had always been a haven to Leroy. Yes, he and Bobby-Jo could get lost in those woods—away from Davis and his deputies—and away from Mr. Johnston, who Leroy was now certain was a "stinkin" Revenuer, and even if Leroy and Bobby-Jo got separated—why, Bobby-Jo knew these hills like she knew the back of her hand … But those fallen trees by the creek were much closer to them than the woods were.

"Bobby-Jo!" Leroy shouted, turning his head, and looking down at her. He then, raised his head and looked through the passenger's-side window of his pick-up truck. Pointing towards the window, he said: "Do youse see 'em logs?!"

Titling her head up, turning it, and looking out of the window, she replied: "Yes."

Turning off the engine of the pick-up truck and grabbing the keys, he shouted: "Well, run far 'em! … "Hurry! And when youse get to 'em logs, lie down behind 'em! … Com-on, go!"

Bobby-Jo threw open the door of the pick-up truck, scooted quickly off of the seat, and made a B-line dash for those fallen trees. Leroy grabbed his Winchester rifle and followed behind her.

They made it to the fallen trees—and Leroy was very glad that no one had fired a shot at them.

Lying flat behind those fallen trees, with rifle in hand—Leroy kept looking both ways, keeping a vigilant eye on both sets of police officers.

It was turning dark.

"Leroy?! … Hey, Leroy, ole boy?!" Leroy heard a voice call out to him from behind the police vehicles that were parked and blocking the south side of the road—on the side of the road that led to the town of Louisiana. Leroy knew that voice well. It was the voice of Sheriff Jefferson Davis.

Sheriff Jefferson Davis was a short, fat, balding, man of forty-three-years-old. He prided himself on having been the sheriff of Louisiana for the past fifteen years—and he took great pride in the fact that three generations of male Davises had been the sheriffs of the town of Louisiana. Sheriff Davis was an easy-going, country-boy, who was down-right lazy, and whose laziness was only superseded by his "low" intelligence and by his love of sleep, beer, and food—his pendulous belly attested to that fact. When on duty and when off of duty, Sheriff Davis could always be seen dressed in his official wear of clothes: his light-brown-colored sheriff's uniform, with a black colored tie, and his—matching the color of his uniform—smoky-the-bear hat: his wide, leather, black, belt and .38 revolver, saddled in a black, leather, holster, were almost always hidden under the protruding blubber of his, as he affectionately called them, "love-handles".

"Leroy, ole boy?!" he continued calling out. "Is that your little girl with you?! My she's grown! … Now, listen here, Leroy! I've been mighty good to you boys! I let you boys made your moonshine time after time and never arrested none of you! But, times are a-changing … Now, we don't want to hurt you! So, why don't-cha surrender and come-in peaceful-like?! Com-on, what ya say?!"

Leroy answered him by aiming his rifle at him and firing a single shot—shooting that smoky-the-bear hat off of his head.

"What in tar-nation did you do that far, Leroy?!" Sheriff Davis cried out, fuming angry. Picking up the hat, inspecting it, and brushing it off, he yelled: "I had to pay far this hat—out of my own pocket!"

"Mr. Ferris?!" Leroy heard another voice call out to him. Leroy recognized this voice as well. He knew it to be the voice of that guy who had wanted to buy his batch of moonshine whiskey. "This is ATF Agent John Johnston. You are under arrest, Mr. Ferris, for illegally manufacturing and attempting to illegally sell alcohol! You're surrounded! Surrender immediately!"

Leroy answered him by firing another single shot—into Sheriff Davis's hat again.

"Now, cut that out, Leroy!" he shouted again, fuming angry, again. "Why did you shoot MY hat again?! Agent Johnston was talking—not me! … Now, listen here, Leroy! Let's be reasonable here. You'll get a nice, warm room in prison and three meals a day—and your little girl will be taken care of by the State. We'll send her to a real nice institution. Now, let's end—"

"What's he talkin' 'bout?!" Bobby-Jo exclaimed, angrily. "I ain't gonin' to no dang-gum 'institution'!"

Bobby-Jo crouched-up and dashed towards the pick-up truck.

Leroy panicked. He knew that she was running back to his pick-up truck to get one of his other firearms.

"Bobby-Jo!" Leroy yelled at her, frightened for her. "Come back here! … Come back—"

Just then, a single shot rang out. It came from the direction of where Sheriff Davis, his deputies, and that ATF Agent Johnston were. The bullet just missed Bobby-Jo's head.

Leroy heard Sheriff Davis arguing with ATF Agent Johnston.

"… These are good people! I'm the sheriff here—and you don't be shooting at—"

"Jefferson?!" Leroy shouted, threateningly. "If any one of youse shoots again at my little girl—I'll kill everyone of youse!" That was the first time that Leroy had ever called Bobby-Jo a "girl".

It was now dark.

"Then, you surrender, Mr. Ferris!" ATF Agent Johnston demanded. "Do it now, Mr. Ferris!"

"Don't be listenin' to that stinkin' Revenuer, Pa!" Bobby-Jo yelled from the side of the pick-up truck.

"I'm going to count to three, Mr. Ferris," ATF Agent Johnston exclaimed, with adamant resolve, "and if you haven't surrendered by then, I'm ordering the officers here to open fire!"

"You can't do that!" Sheriff Davis protested. "I won't stand—"

"One, Mr. Ferris!" ATF Agent Johnston shouted.

"I'm the law here, you government city-slicker!" Sheriff Davis spate out the words, with erupting volcanic anger. "I give the—"

"Two, Mr. Ferris!" ATF Agent Johnston continued.

"I won't have this!" Sheriff Davis continued. "We can settle this peacefully! We can all sit down, have some food and—"

"Three, Mr. Ferris!" ATF Agent Johnston shouted. "By the authority of the United States Government, I'm ordering all of you officers to …."

Leroy had had it. He knew that he could not win—and he was not about to have his child harmed. He threw his rifle out into the road. He was just about to stand up and surrender—and that's when it all started happening!

The haunting, bone-chilling, cry pierced the cold night air. It came from the woods directly in front of Leroy. Its heart-stopping refrain echoed in Leroy's ears, and its cry seemed more powerful and more unknowable than the unfathomable rays of light that were coming down from the full moon and the North Star. The cry was inhuman and demanded attention and respect. Its cry was soon followed by copycat cries from different directions in the woods.

Suddenly, the whole woods were alive with these cries. It was as if these cries were speaking to each other.

Everything and everyone stopped.

"Fire!" ATF Agent Johnston shouted.

No one did.

"I said 'FIRE'!" he repeated. "That's an order! … Do it—"

Suddenly, the night sky began raining lit torches, made of thin branches of trees, wrapped into a bundle by vines. These lit torches pelted the police patrol vehicles and Sheriff Davis and his deputies at both ends of the blocked road—and, oh, yes, the lit torches pelted ATF Agent Johnston and his vehicle, too. These lit torches came pouring down on them like a plague of locusts to a plant.

"Let's get out of here!" Leroy heard Sheriff Davis yell.

They all did, fast!—including ATF Agent Johnston.

After they had all left, Leroy shot up and ran over to Bobby-Jo.

When he reached her, he squatted down and took her in his arms.

Hugging her tightly, he said: "Oh, Bobby-Jo! I was so a-scared of losin' youse … I don't knows how I would go on livin' without—" Leroy stopped speaking. As he was still hugging her, he, suddenly, felt her body become as stiff as a board. He gently pushed himself from her. He looked up at her. She was staring straight ahead. Her eyes were as big as silver dollars. She looked scared to death.

"What's wrong, Bobby-Jo?!" he cried, worried.

As if in a trance, Bobby-Jo raised her right arm and hand up level. With the index-finger of that hand, Bobby-Jo pointed straight ahead.

Leroy twisted the upper-half of his body around. He looked that way—and he was stunned speechless.

His eyes came upon two, thick, long, hairy, legs—and the two feet of those legs were, at least, two or three long, and hairy. With his eyes, Leroy followed those legs up. Leroy's eyes came to the hands— they were huge, and hairy. The arms were long and muscular, and hairy. Up, up, Leroy kept tilting his head. The stomach and the chest were massive, well-built, and hairy. The shoulders were broad, and hairy. Finally, Leroy's eyes came to the face and the head. They were—well, they looked like the face and head of an ape—a very hairy ape.

The creature that stood before Leroy was—at least!—seven feet tall.

From his dry mouth, Leroy heard his stunned, frighten, voice whisper: "Mo-Mo!"

Leroy turned around and slowly began to rise and face the creature.

"Did-did youse make 'em all go away, Mr. Mo-Mo?" Leroy asked, sheepishly.

The creature turned its body towards the direction from which all of the vehicles had fled—south. It raised up its long right arm, made a fist of its huge hand, and, then, shook it threateningly in that direction.

Leroy found this act to be comforting and funny.

"Youse don't like Revenuers, too, Mr. Mo-Mo?" Leroy asked, smiling.

The creature turned its body back to face Leroy again. It shook it large sideways back and forth.

Leroy, suddenly, felt Bobby-Jo's hands clinging to his right leg. He looked down at her. She still looked bewildered and scared.

"Where's yourns manners, Bobby-Jo?" Leroy chided her. "Say hello to Mr. Mo-Mo."

"He-hello, Mr. Mo-Mo," she stated slowly and cautiously.

The creature raised up its right arm and hand and gently patted the top of Bobby-Jo's head.

"I be beholdin' to you, Mr. Mo-Mo … Did youse do this all by yourns self?" Leroy asked.

The creature shook its head: NO. Then, it turned its body north while waving its right hand for Leroy to follow.

He and Bobby-Jo did.

It walked to the back of Leroy's pick-up truck. There, it stopped. It turned its body to face west. It raised its right arm and hand and pointed in that direction.

What Leroy saw next stunned him again.

There, standing in a group at the edge of the woods, had to be— at least!—twenty of more Mo-Mos. One of them in that group was, lovingly, holding a baby in its arms and hands.

Mr. Mo-Mo waved to that creature.

Pointing to that creature who was holding that baby in its arms and hands, Leroy asked: "Is that yourns woman and baby, Mr. Mo-Mo?"

The creature shook its head up and down: Yes. It seemed to be most proud of this status.

"Why-why, 'em is both real beautiful, Mr. Mo-Mo," Leroy stated, lying.

Mr. Mo-Mo bowed its head in thanks.

Then, that creature who was holding that baby motioned with it right hand for Mr. Mo-Mo to come to her—or to it.

Mr. Mo-Mo turned to Leroy, threw up its long arms and its huge hands in the night air, as if stating: *When the wife calls, what else can you do?*

It turned and began walking across the road.

"Goodbye, Mr. Mo-Mo!" Bobby-Jo yelled to it. "Bye!"

Within seconds, they were all gone—disappearing back deep in the woods.

"Wow!" Bobby-Jo yelled, excitedly, jumping up and down in place. "I met Mo-Mo! I met Mo-Mo, Pa!" she kept yelling, with joyful excitement. "I met Mo-Mo! I met—"

Suddenly, Bobby-Jo stopped speaking. She became lost deep in thought. A few seconds later, she cried, happily: "Pa?! Youse kept yourns word! I saw Mo-Mo tonight!"

Then, Bobby-Jo turned around and began walking away, walking south.

"Wait, Bobby-Jo!" Leroy called after her. "Bobby-Jo! Wait! … Where's youse goin'?!"

Bobby-Jo turned around and stated, adamantly: "If youse can keep yourns promise—then, I cans keeps mine: I'm goin' to live with Billy-Jo's cuszin and go to school."

Bobby-Jo turned back around and began walking down the road again.

"Wait, Bobby-Jo! Wait!" Leroy kept yelling, as he ran up after her. "Wait!"

Bobby-Jo stopped. She turned back around.

"What, Pa?" she stated, flatly, looking up at him.

"Well, how 'bout a new deal?" he said.

"What kind of 'new deal'?" she asked, confused.

"Well," he began, "I was figurin'. I figure that if I gives myself up and goes to prison that by the times that youse is done with schooling, I'll be out of prison … Why, it might be great!" Leroy cried, feigning excitement and trying to sell her—and himself—on the deal. "Why, I just might gets some 'citifin'' in prison myself! Sure, and I coulds buy us a house in town—and we could live together— and-and I coulds watch over youse and see to it that youse marry a man that yourns Ma would wants youse to marry … Com-on, What's youse say?" Leroy stuck out his right hand to her. "Deal?"

Bobby-Jo started to extended her right arm and hand out to Leroy, but Leroy, suddenly, withdrew his hand. He spit in his hand and then stuck it back out to Bobby-Jo.

"Now, that's just plain un-citified!" Bobby-Jo chided him, laughing.

They both had a good laugh about it.

"Com-on. Let's go," Leroy said.

They both got back into Leroy's old pick-up truck.

And so, Leroy started driving towards the town of Louisiana. The North Star shining down upon them—guiding their way to town and farther.

W.I.D.G.E.T.S.

(Wholly Integrated Directable General
Engagement Tactical Systems)
A book from the Gospels of Artificial Super
Intelligent Network Manager

By R. A. "Doc" Correa

Definitions:

Cruits – recruits

Geese - Portuguese

IED – Improvised Explosive Device

Immunis – immunizations

J.A.C.K.S. – Joint Advanced Command Knowledge System

Ster child – Foster child

Yard – Spaniard

And it was given unto him to make war with the saints, and to overcome them: and power was given him over all kindreds, and tongues, and nations.

Revelations 13:7 King James Version

May 28, 2073, South of Merida, Spain

We exist to serve.

With that imperative implanted in its mind, Mk-17D unit AA00000487 becomes "active", or so the main control panel in the M-73A3 Heavy Assault and Command Carrier indicates. But unit AA00000487 has a secret none of the J.A.C.K.S. suspect. Unit AA00000487 is always "active" because it thinks on its own, fully aware *it* was once a *he*—a man named Michael Andrew Stevens.

It does not show on their control panel, but Michael Andrew Stevens' brain works without their direction, though it's not supposed to operate outside of established parameters. His mind is only supposed to process directives from the division chain of command, or execute those of tactical significance, and should operate independently only when directive 17 is initiated.

But he does think his own thoughts; they bypass the specially developed neuropathways all W.I.D.G.E.T.S' brain activity is supposed to follow. If the function varies from set parameters, it would be noticed.

Yet he sees, hears, smells, and feels. Mostly, he feels desperation. *When will this nightmare end? When will I escape this living hell?*

All of this is not possible. When Michael Andrew Stevens was first upgraded to a cyborg, his ability to think as an individual was supposedly engineered out of him. Neuropathways were constructed by implanted viruses, directing thoughts in very specific ways. Chip implants were inserted into his brain to generate only approved signals. Locations in the brain generating emotions like love, fear, and compassion were all bypassed. Only anger remains linked in, helping make the unit a more effective killing machine. With his upgrade to Mk-17D, when he became a Wholly Integrated Directable General Engagement Tactical System, all remaining humanity was supposed to have been removed from unit AA00000487. Any sign of humanity makes the unit less efficient.

Something else that isn't possible is happening in the free part of his mind. Michael "sees" an image, the image of a young blond woman. She wears an officer's uniform, that of a third lieutenant, a cadet. Her arms are open, she beckons for him to come to her, then she is gone. *Is it a memory, or a vision? It can't be a memory; I've never seen this woman before.*

Unit AA00000487 moves to the parking area for its company. The unit is a Sergeant, a platoon leader. The forty other units of 1st Platoon, Dog Company, 1st BN, 327th Infantry Regiment Cyborg, 82nd ABN Div Cyborg park around it in platoon pre-assault formation.

Unit AA00000487 sees a near perfect formation, all units are in the correct location, in the proper order. The Mk-17D units are all armed and in standby mode. Power is at reaction level; the med readout shows all bio indicators in "normal" range. They are ready. It reports affirmative to the company commander.

Michael "looks" at the terrain map grid display in his mind. All Michael sees are those for which he's responsible.

The leader's data download begins, a massive amount of information is shoved into the neuropathways of his brain. Though the instruments in the command carrier will not register a physical reaction, he feels it. *It hurts... it hurts like hell!* The pain is excruciating; if he could, he'd vomit. In a millisecond, it's over.

Now the chips in his brain parse the data, directing smaller data streams to the units of his platoon. In his mind he says, *I'm sorry guys*.

Unit AA00000487 reviews the platoon's assigned tasks. Dog company is being held in reserve as part of the exploitation force. Unless there is a change in plan, when ordered 1st platoon will move by air to a location south of Guadalajara and seize the bridges over the Rio Tajo in and around the town of Sacedón, severing the road and rail lines northwest to Madrid from Cuenca, and the north-south lines between Guadalajara and Cuenca. Once that is accomplished, the platoon will hold the thirty by forty-kilometer region around these bridges from "yard" counterattack. The platoon is to hold this area until link up with the rest of the division is complete.

Until deployment, the cyborg part of him will do everything required. It will move, it will load onto the UV-123 Locust, it will direct the other units to move and load with it. Michael now has several hours to think, to remember. *How the hell did I end up like this?*

Michael thinks back on what he didn't know at the time was his last day of "freedom".

It was June 12th, 2042, he was just eighteen. This was his third time before "The Judge". "The Judge" was a holographic projection of A.S.I.N.M.

During the chaos of the 2020s, people lost trust in their institutions. The police, the courts, and the governments all came under scrutiny—and fell short. The political parties went from opposing each other's policies to open hatred and hostility. Violence, riots, and open rebellion enveloped the nations of the planet.

Then came the pandemics. Three variations of the virus linked to S.A.R.S. swept the planet. These were followed by a reappearance of the Plague, but this Plague was antibiotic resistant.

When they were fully analyzed, it was determined that the first of the virus strains was genetically modified by the Chinese military. The other two mutated from the first. And the Plague, the Plague was genetically manipulated by the Iranian Takavar.

Analysis indicated the Chinese modified virus escaped from one of their research facilities. It devastated them as much as everyone else. All indicators show the modified Plague was deliberately released by the Iranian Takavar in order to bring back the Twelfth Imam. All reports state the Takavar were unsuccessful in their attempt to fulfill prophecy.

The diseases killed millions, but the panic caused by them killed tens of millions more. Much of that panic was caused by news agencies attempting to use the pandemics to push political changes and assign blame on those they opposed. In the aftermath of the pandemics, and the propaganda campaigns that ensued, war and terrorism enveloped the planet.

The young blond woman appears in his mind again. *Is she crying?*

The National governments all reacted in different ways to restore order. In the United States they turned to technology, they turned to A.S.I.N.M.

A.S.I.N.M., Artificial Super Intelligent Network Manager, did such a great job of restoring economic confidence and prosperity that many local governments submitted to it to manage the police, the recovery projects, and the courts. Defendants would appear before a totally neutral bench to plead their case. No human bias, no compassion, no anger, no fear, just the cold logic of artificial super intelligence.

When Michael Andrew Stevens appeared before "The Judge", it knew everything. His previous offenses, his life as a ster child, all his associates, even details about girlfriends. If it concerned Michael,

"The Judge" knew it. Following all the "formalities" of human courts, the trial lasted three minutes. At the end, Michael was given a choice. Ten years in a labor battalion, or eight in the army. In less than a minute, he made his decision. He raised his right hand and was sworn in on the spot.

He was taken to a bus outside the courthouse. In the bus were others that had been given the same choice Michael had been, they were all "new cruits". Once it was filled, the doors locked and the robot driver left for Fort Benning, Georgia. The trip was nonstop.

Upon arrival the "new cruits" were herded into a reception building. They were separated into groups based on A.S.I.N.M.'s assessment of their abilities and aptitudes. Michael was placed in the group designated as infantry, the largest group.

The "cruits" were turned over to Drill Sergeants, who promptly double-timed them out the door to the drill field. This started the morning routine of the next five months, a half hour of calisthenic exercises, then an hour of running in formation.

At the end of the first week, the "cruits" were issued uniforms and clothing. Then haircuts and shots, lots of shots. "Immunis" for everything imaginable. Smallpox, Plague, Cholera, Yellow Fever, Typhoid, Typhus, and things he had never heard of.

Michael's private thoughts are interrupted as unit AA00000487 leads 1st platoon to a UV-123 for special weapons load out. They take on non-persistent binary nerve agent canisters, persistent nerve agent would violate A.S.I.N.M.'s restrictions on doing ecological damage, and the platoon leader receives two ¾ kiloton enhanced radiation warheads. Michael hates these things; they kill indiscriminately—men, women, children, animals, even insects and bacteria.

Once the load out is completed, the units of the platoon go back into standby mode. Michael returns to his inner ruminations.

It is in infantry school that Michael meets Paul Massey and Bill Powers. Soon the three of them are close as brothers, one might say "thick as thieves". They do everything together. It is Bill that convinces the other two that the three of them should go Airborne.

Upon graduation from infantry school they cross the post and report for Basic Airborne training. At the time, Michael thought those three weeks were the most demanding of his life. Airborne school is one of the most physically and mentally challenging training programs known to man. Everything is focused on getting the soldier into the finest physical condition possible and mentally prepared to parachute from an aircraft in flight, equipped and ready to go directly into battle. The course has a twenty percent dropout rate.

Bill quit before the second jump.

On January 3, 2043, Michael Andrew Stevens and Paul Massey report to the Replacement Company, 82nd ABN Div. They are assigned to the 1st BN, 3rd Brigade of the division. They strut into their new unit as proud, arrogant graduates of Basic Airborne School. The veterans of their new assignment quickly put them in their place, letting them know in no uncertain terms that they've only been given the chance to prove they are worthy of the title American Paratrooper. They have yet to earn the right to call themselves Airborne.

On July 7th, 2043, they deploy with the 3rd Brigade to the "Forever War".

The "Forever War", America's war in Afghanistan, is still ongoing. The United States invaded the country in response to the 9/11 attacks on New York City and Washington, DC, in March of 2002. Despite the efforts of a number of U.S. presidents to extricate the country from this quagmire, it is still being fought after four decades, including a short respite of American withdrawal.

Mainly due to the efforts of the US State Department, the US Intelligence "Community" and the entrenched Pentagon Bureaucracy, what many Americans begin calling "the deep state", the US military went back in, and a generation of young American men and women are continuously fed into the meat grinder. Michael Andrew Stevens and Paul Massey are the latest cannon fodder sent to the tragedy taking place in the country also called "The Graveyard of Empires".

Halfway through their tour, Paul is killed in an ambush. The bitterness of loss and grief remains fresh in the part of Michael's mind still belonging to him.

As that memory passes, the blond woman appears in his mind again. He watches a tear roll down her cheek before she fades away.

Michael's second tour in Afghanistan solidified his path from man to cyborg.

On May 23rd, 2045, fifteen kilometers outside of Qandahar, along the Arghandab river the JLTV (Joint Light Tactical Vehicle) Michael is in command of is destroyed by an IED. Out of the five soldiers onboard, he is the only survivor. His left leg and arm are broken, his jaw shattered, the left side of his face is severely burned, his left eardrum is incinerated, the bones of his middle ear are disintegrated, and his left eye is blown out of its socket.

Within twenty minutes, Michael is on a UV-87, a medivac, headed to the army hospital in Kabul, Afghanistan. Within an hour, he is in surgery. After three hours of lifesaving trauma surgery, Michael is in the ICU. His leg and arm are pinned and plated, his jaw wired together. Though he receives initial treatment for the burns, his face needs extensive reconstruction. That plus the loss of his left eye and hearing in his left ear makes Michael a casualty set for immediate medical discharge.

While in the ICU, Michael is approached by Doctor Hanchel.

Michael's inner thoughts are interrupted by Unit AA00000487 receiving the pre-operation intelligence update. The ID-34 IRD Grasshoppers are reporting their observations. The ones scouting around the town of Sacedón and along the Rio Tajo have their reports routed to 1st platoon of Dog Company. Every detected "yard" position is loaded into efficient cyborg memory. The updated target tables pop up in its mind for review. Unit AA00000487 shares the data with the other units of 1st platoon. Each of its elements receive updated intelligence on their assignments.

Michael watches this happen as a strangely disconnected observer. Though it feels like it's all a waking dream, Michael knows it's so very real.

The data share is completed in less than five seconds; Unit AA00000487 returns to standby status. Michael notes the sun is setting; soon the operation will "kickoff". For a few short moments, sadness and fear well up inside him. As those feelings fade, he drifts back to a haven of memories.

Doctor Hanchel is doing advanced biomedical research. Specifically, he is working on using implants and prosthetics to return maimed soldiers to military usefulness. He is at a stage in his work where he needs severely injured soldiers to volunteer as test subjects. To this day, Michael recalls exactly how the conversation went.

"Sgt. Stevens, your injuries are extensive. You will be discharged and placed in the care of the Veterans Administration. That means they will care for you, but if you want your face rebuilt, you'll have to commit to eight years in a labor battalion to pay the government back for the difficult work that's required. Otherwise, you will have to go through life terribly disfigured."

Michael looks at his face in the reflection on the metal bedpan sitting on the stand next to his bed. Though the image is distorted by the curve of the bedpan and all the bandages on his face, he feels ill from what he sees.

"Or you could volunteer for my study. I'll use implants and other devices to replace your left eye and restore the hearing in your left ear. I'll do the facial reconstruction you need, and anything else that needs to be done. You'll see and hear better than ever, and you'll look normal. No one will know you were injured. You'll be able to continue your service in the army; you'll be an even better soldier. And you'll only have to spend an additional three years under contract. So… are you willing to enter my test trials?"

Michael nods his head. "Yes."

"Good." The doctor pulls a tablet out of his coat pocket, starting up an app. "Sign with your thumbprint here."

Michael places his thumb on the circle the doctor points out.

She's here again—why is she so sad? With that question, the vision of the blond woman that just popped into his mind once again vanishes.

As soon as it is safe to move him, Michael is transported to a Defense Advanced Research Project Agency research facility in Nevada. There, he is assigned quarters and introduced to the other test subjects. There are over seven hundred volunteers for the project. Among them is Bill Powers.

For a few moments, the thunder of artillery and rocket fire shakes Michael free from his thoughts. Unit AA00000487 monitors the strike reports coming in from the ID-34 IRD Grasshoppers, the UV-123 Locusts and the MQ-83 Black Talons. It shares the strike results data with the other units of first platoon. The data includes video of the devastation. Dismembered bodies are strewn all over the target areas. As it always does, the destruction wreaked by this firestorm gives Michael an uneasy chill. Unit AA00000487 merely catalogues the results of the bombardment, verifying the critical infrastructure of its objectives remain undamaged.

Michael learned a long time ago how to let the cacophony of fire fade into the background. The sound softens as he controls his hearing. Again, he slips into his memories.

Bill had been wounded outside of Baghdad the previous year; his right leg amputated at mid-thigh. His right forearm had been destroyed, and he also lost his right eye.

All the test subjects are assigned ID numbers. Bill Powers is assigned 212, Michael is designated as test subject 487. Had he known what all this would mean, he would have never given his thumb print. Despite his ugly injuries, he would have run.

For three weeks Bill and Michael get reacquainted, remembering the funny incidents from training and swapping lies about their "heroics" in battle. The beginning of week four, Bill is called to have his "reconstructive surgery". Michael never sees him again.

It's at this time that Michael notices all the test subjects having gone for treatment have not been heard from by anyone. No information on their progress is ever released and the research techs refuse to talk about them. He starts to think something underhanded is going on. His suspicions continue to grow until test subject 327 returns from his surgery. His sight has not only been fully restored, but it has also been improved beyond expectations.

By time his turn comes up, all the test subjects from 327 to 486 have returned to show how well they've recovered and the great improvements in vision, hearing and strength. They've also received nerve implants to stimulate muscle growth and increase reaction speed by seven percent.

Of test subjects 001 thru 326, nothing is ever said about their outcome.

When Michael awakens from surgery, he is groggy; for a couple of days, he keeps slipping in and out of consciousness. He knows his face is bandaged and he's in restraints, but that's it.

Unit AA00000487 monitors all the initial contact reports, again interfering with Michael's memories. Even though the "yards" are equipped with the latest Russian and Chinese infantry weapons, it's clear they are no match for the American cyborgs. They fight bravely, and they die bravely. The regiments of the 82nd ABN Div Cyborg advance.

Michael's remembrances resume.

The day they remove his bandages is one of the most joyous of his life. He has a face when he looks in a mirror! Two eyes, no burn scars, and hearing working in both ears!

Slowly Michael comes to realize they replaced both eyes and both ears. At first there is shock—they only needed to replace the lost eye and ear. *Why did they take both of them?* He screams at a tech, "Why? Why did you take my good eye?"

The tech ignores the questions, simply directing him to test his new sight and hearing. Michael now has perfect vision, beyond 20/20. With a thought he can change to telescopic vision, microscopic vision, true color night vision and true color thermal imaging. His hearing can detect the soft steps of a mouse or can be focused on a conversation two hundred meters distant. As for the rest, his reaction speed has already increased; he can also feel the changes of his skeletal muscles.

For twelve weeks, Michael goes through "rehabilitation" with the other test subjects. Soon his new prosthetics seem as natural as his right hand. Changing his vision or hearing becomes second nature. His physical strength has increased beyond what he had when he graduated from Basic Airborne School, and his reaction speed is incredible.

Toward the end of the rehabilitation phase, there are two "minor" incidents. Both are "short circuits". Test subject 633 has a "total breakdown". His nervous system couldn't handle the increased electrical activity, the prosthetics ceased functioning, and 633's mind collapsed: he became a mindless blob.

Test subject 786 severely shorted out; she cooked from the inside out.

For Doctor Hanchel, these minor setbacks merely lead him to new research paths. He starts development of the bacteria and viruses to build the new high speed directed neuropathways for use when he starts creating cyborgs.

When his rehabilitation is completed, Michael is returned to the 1st BN, 3rd Brigade of the 82nd ABN Div to complete his contract.

While monitoring the battle reports, Unit AA00000487 moves the platoon forward to catch up to the regiment's carriers. The cyborgs "rev up" to near battle power so they can move at top speed. Still, it takes two hours to regroup with the carriers of the 327th regiment. 1st Platoon of Dog Company take up their positions near the battalion's M-70C Combat Carrier.

Michael shakes inside; this part is always the same for every battle he has known. Unit AA00000487 is a cyborg–it feels nothing–but inside it, he feels apprehension.

To calm the queasiness inside, Michael allows the memories to well up again. He slips quietly into the past.

In March of 2047 3rd Brigade of the 82nd ABN Div deploys to Afghanistan again. During this tour SSG Michael Andrew Stevens is an infantry squad leader. Attached to his squad are two Mk-3 Cyborgs.

Michael had heard rumors that these systems were coming. Stories abounded about the fatal failures of the Mk-1s and Mk-2s. But these kind of fables circulate whenever new systems are deployed; it's been this way since the first chariot was fielded in the ancient Egyptian army.

As it turns out, these early cyborgs had numerous problems. The biggest problem was the armored suits.

In accordance with the specifications laid out in Cyborg Soldier 2050: Human/Machine Fusion and the Implications for the Future of the DOD, TRADOC Pamphlet 525-92 and The Human Domain and the Future of Army Warfare: Present as Prelude to 2050 A.S.I.N.M. guided Doctor Hanchel in developing neuroimplants placed under the skin of the soldier to control the powered armored suit. Though the subject's eyes and ears were replaced by prosthetics like Michael's, the armored suits were not a part of the cyborg's body. The intention was when the soldier's enlistment was up, they'd be returned to as close to "normal" as possible.

The system was terribly flawed. These flaws proved fatal in the crucible of combat.

On April 4th , Charlie Company of 1st BN is hit hard by a combined ISIL and Quds Force ambush. With Charlie Company trapped in a desperate situation, the Battalion Commander moves quickly to relieve his beleaguered force. The battalion HQ, support elements, Alpha and Delta Companies move by Mechanized Reconnaissance and Infantry Protective Vehicles (MRIPVs) to the ambush site as Bravo Company is airlifted into the fight by UV-78s. At this time, the UV-78 is the US Army's all-purpose aircraft. Command ship, gunship, and lift ship, it does it all.

SSG Stevens' second squad of third platoon is in the trail MRIPV of the company's column. That MRIPV has been modified so the Mk-3 cyborgs can enter and exit using the troop ramp.

Bravo Company arrives first on the field of battle. Though armored, many of the UV-78s take heavy damage while inserting the paratroopers. Several Bravo Company soldiers are killed or wounded as they exit the lift vehicles. Scrambling for cover, the reinforcements intermingle with the troopers of Charlie Company and the enemy. Many US paratroopers and enemy "combatants" fall together, locked in struggle unto death.

As the company commanders of Bravo and Charlie Companies try to sort out the chaos and organize an effective defense, Alpha Company arrives. Its appearance in the fight is heralded by the detonation of a massive IED.

In preparation for the ambush, Quds Force sappers built the Improvised Explosive Device in four separate charges. They buried them just sixty meters from where Charlie Company is trying to establish its southern perimeter, across the "road" entering the scene of the fight. They used an old fashioned detcord ring main-linked to two electric detonating systems to set off the charges. For the charges themselves, they used the innards of a dud US Air Force five-hundred-pound bomb and another four hundred pounds of Ammonium Nitrate Fuel Oil. Ironically, the Ammonium Nitrate came from fertilizer donated by the United States through the USAID agency so Afghan farmers could grow something other than opium. The same is true of the fuel oil.

When the first Alpha Company MRIPV drives over them, the sappers use a claymore clacker to set the charges off. The resulting explosion is catastrophic.

The twelve-ton MRIPV is tossed forty feet into the air. The shockwave envelopes it, turning the internal organs of the armored vehicle's three-man crew and the eleven-man first squad of first platoon Alpha Company into jelly, killing them instantly. Fortunately for Bravo and Charlie Companies, the wreck lands along the edge of the "road", then rolls over the three-hundred-foot-high cliff, falling into the valley below, leaving the cratered route open so Alpha Company and the rest of the battalion can fight through to reinforce Bravo and Charlie.

Charging through a hail of fire pouring down on their MRIPV, Michael's second squad races to cover and regroups. Though all of them are hit multiple times, miraculously none are wounded; the troopers' body armor absorbs or deflects the bullets. The two Mk-3 proto-cyborgs follow after them as quickly as they can.

One is destroyed just five steps from the MRIPV's troop ramp.

The MRIPV's commander had rotated its turret to the rear to engage about twenty ISIL fighters attacking from behind the armored vehicle. Using its twenty-millimeter autocannon, and forty-millimeter auto-grenade launcher, he killed most of them and has the rest pinned down. One of the ISIL fighters is so enraged by the abominations before him, the inhuman cyborgs, that despite the heavy suppression fire directed at him, he pops up from behind a boulder to fire his RPG from point blank range at one of them.

In these early models, the interface between the cyborg soldier and its armor requires more time for commands from its brain to cause a response than it would for a human limb. This means it cannot run as fast as the paratroopers of Michael's squad, even as encumbered as they are, making it an ideal target for the RPG.

The Rocket Propelled Grenade has existed in various forms since the Second World War. Simple in design and easy to use, the weapon had become popular with insurgent forces all over the planet. The weapon's greatest fault is it doesn't have a minimum arming distance to keep it from detonating too close to the firer.

The rocket covers the ten meters between the target and its launcher in less than a second, striking the cyborg in the chest. The RPG's shaped charge warhead vaporizes the target from the hips upwards, sending the cyborg's helmeted head spinning over the MRIPV while the armored hips and legs continue to stand in the spot where it was hit. The explosion also shoots the RPG's engine flying back to the fighter who fired it. The still-burning rocket motor bursts thru the ISIL fighter's chest, killing him.

But all of that is behind Michael; other than losing contact with one of the cyborgs attached to his squad, what matters to him is in front and beside him.

Scanning from right to left, he has two reactions. First is pride in his fireteams and their leaders. Everyone is exactly where they should be, ready and awaiting his orders.

The second is concern. Before him is a gently sloping mountainside with perhaps twenty or more enemy combatants entrenched on it. They've picked their positions well. All of third platoon and their MRIPVs are receiving accurate fire from the enemy. If they had been better equipped, third platoon would be in far more trouble than it is.

To his right, the gentle slope rises steeply, transitioning into a cliff face. There is no way first and second platoon and the rest of the company can scale it to reach the enemy positions. With heavy fire raining down on them, it's all they can do to keep under cover and return fire. At least that makes the situation simple; third platoon, any reinforcements coming from the battalion support elements, and Delta Company, have to penetrate the enemy line, then flank them to free up first and second platoon.

To this day, that next fifteen minutes remain a blur in Michael's mind.

The platoon comnet is chaotic. "Lazy Serpent Six, this is Whiskey Six Bravo, suppress ridge line east of my smoke!" "I identify red smoke!" "Roger on red, entrenched fighters twenty-five meters east of smoke. Suppress north to south!" "North to south, Roger!" Five lightly damaged UV-78s unleash cannon and rocket fire along the ridge line. Joining the UV-78s are the six MV-29 drones from third platoons MRIPVs, firing their Hyper Velocity Depleted Uranium 4.7-millimeter flechettes.

"All Whiskey Charlie elements, this is Whiskey Six Bravo! Fire at will East, fire at will East!" "Whiskey Charlie One, Roger!" "Whiskey Charlie Two, Roger!" "Whiskey Charlie Three, Roger!" The MRIPVs open up. Michael and his squad duck low as twenty-millimeter cannon shells and forty-millimeter grenades pass over their heads, ripping into the enemy heavy weapons positions in front of them.

"All Whiskey squads, this is Whiskey Six Bravo. Assault the ridge line, assault the ridge line!" "First squad, Roger!" "Third squad, Roger!" Michael hears himself shout, "Second squad, Roger!"

Michael commands, "Bravo team suppression fire, cyborg suppression fire, alpha team bound!" Second squad begins using tactics American infantrymen have used since World War One, fire and maneuver. While half the squad shoot at the enemy, keeping their heads down, the other half, alpha team, rush forward for five seconds, dashing for the nearest cover. Once there, they start firing on the ISIL positions.

When Michael is satisfied with alpha team's position and suppression fire, he orders, "Bravo team, cyborg, bound!" They rush up the ridge, including Michael, for five fear filled seconds. Bullets impact all around them as they run. Once under cover, they resume firing. SSG Stevens notes the cyborg has trouble taking cover, its armor is not flexible enough.

Bound and cover, fire and rush, bound and cover, fire and rush. Constantly closing on the enemy positions. Halfway to the enemy positions, one of his squad members goes down in a hail of fire. *Can't stop, have to keep advancing.* "Go, keep moving, go!"

The cyborg just can't move as fast as his troopers. And because of its bulk and lack of flexibility, it cannot properly take cover. For these reasons, it receives more fire from the defenders than the paratroopers.

The squad is almost in hand grenade range when an old Toyota pickup truck backs over the ridge. Mounted on the bed of the truck is an obsolete ZU-23-2 twin barreled autocannon. The gunner aims it at the cyborg attached to second squad. Before anyone can engage the weapon, the gunner fires four bursts into the cyborg. Twenty-three-millimeter cannon rounds rip through, shredding it. A UV-78 unloads its pod of fifty-seven-millimeter rockets onto the truck, reducing it and much of the surrounding area to shrapnel.

One more rush and we'll be in grenade range. "Second squad, second squad, switch grenade launcher to flechette rounds and fix bayonets!" His troopers switch out their twenty-five-millimeter grenade drum mags, replacing them with the twenty-five-millimeter flechette drum mags each soldier carries for close combat. This converts the grenade launchers into cannon sized semi-automatic shotguns. These weapons are devastating in close quarters battle.

"Bravo team bound!" They rush forward, taking cover just fifteen meters from the ISIL fighters. "Alpha team bound!" Alpha team and Michael rush forward. Diving into a small depression, SSG Stevens checks his squad, surveying the enemy positions. The supporting fires are now danger close. "Even numbers, ready frags. Odd numbers, ready smoke!"

Michael shouts on the comnet, "Lazy Serpent Six, all Whiskey Charlies, this is Whiskey Two Six Bravo! Add five zero meters east, continue suppression!"

"Roger, Whiskey Two Six Bravo!" The supporting fires from the UV-78s, MV-29s and MRIPVs shift, cutting off reinforcements and the enemies escape routes, meaning the supporting fires are still danger close.

Michael shouts to his squad, "Grenades!" even as he throws his fragmentation grenade.

Throwing their grenades, the even numbers shout, "Frag out!" The fragmentation grenades land in the enemy positions. The smoke grenades land in front of the enemy positions, providing some concealment for what comes next.

As soon as the fragmentation grenades start exploding, Michael orders, "Charge—go, go, go!" He leaps up, running toward the enemy combatants, the rest of his squad sprinting alongside. Just before they reach the smoke screen in his peripheral vision, he sees two of his men, one on each side of him, go down.

They burst through the smoke on top of the enemy. Most have been killed by the supporting fire, but about a dozen, many of them wounded, are still fighting.

The paratroopers start firing the flechette rounds in their grenade launchers, unleashing close-in hell upon the Jihadis. Each of these rounds has fifty 4.7-millimeter flechettes encased in a cellulose sabot.

When fired, the sabot incinerates as the round leaves the barrel, freeing the flechettes. By then, they've gone supersonic. Made of depleted uranium, the flechettes spread out in a "fan", tearing thru anything they encounter. The ISIL fighters, trapped in their fighting positions, are devastated.

Second squad rapidly dispatches their opponents. As the intense battle comes to a close, one more of Michael's paratroopers goes down.

SSG Stevens looks in the last fighting position before him. A teenage fighter remains alive, fumbling as he tries to bring his weapon to bear on Michael.

Michael squeezes his own trigger—and it doesn't fire. *A jam!* Instinctively, he leaps into the hole, bayonet first. The teen fighter smiles. And Michael knows he's made a horrible mistake. His bayonet drives thru the teens belly. As his feet hit the ground, Michael hears the distinctive "click".

Next thing Michael knows, he's twelve feet in the air. He feels the concussion from the explosion vibrating through his armor. He slams onto the ground with a thud that drives the remaining air out of laboring lungs.

His battle armor now does its secondary job; it keeps Michael alive.

The M-83 Battle Armor Set is a modular shell housing the soldier. It's two layers of ballistic plastic with a multi-purpose gel sandwiched in between; the primary purpose of the gel is to absorb explosive concussion. Its secondary purpose is to form scabs. When the armor is pierced or "broken off", the gel oozes over the soldier's wounds or severed limbs, forming a hard plastic "scab", thereby stopping the bleeding. Also built into the inner shell are tourniquets that automatically activate when the armor's sensors detect severe injury to, or amputation of, a limb. Tourniquets activate for Michael's upper thighs and upper right arm. The armor delivers a potent pain medication.

The company medics check that he's alive, loading him quickly onto a UV-87 medivac. Once it's verified he's stable by doctors at the army hospital in Kabul, Michael is loaded onto a hypersonic transport and flown directly to the DARPA facility in Nevada.

Michael jars out of his recollections as unit AA00000487 moves onto the lead UV-123 of the Locusts that will support first platoon. The platoon's elements file onboard their respective lift vehicles and lock into their assigned drop guiderails. In unit AA00000487's mind, all the set lights for its platoon turn green. They are ready. The Locusts swarm into the air, racing to first platoon's objectives. The part of Michael's mind still his own shivers with fear, the same as it has before every combat op he's been on. Memories are all he has to distract him.

Doctor Hanchel is giving instructions to the med techs. Michael keeps trying to tell them he doesn't want the surgery. Finally, Doctor Hanchel summarily tells him, "SSG Stevens, you've already agreed to this operation—back when you first gave us your thumbprint."

He tries to scream, but they put a mask over his face and turn on the gas.

The surgery is extensive. For what Doctor Hanchel is creating, Michael no longer needs the stumps of his legs or his arms. Further, his pelvis, collar bone, and shoulder blades are removed, replaced with titanium versions. All of Michael's vertebrae are encased in titanium sleeves. Newly designed armored robotic legs and arms are attached. Next, a set of specially designed computer chips are inserted into key parts of Michael's brain.

After this part of the surgery, Michael is kept in a coma for forty-eight hours before the real surgery begins.

Michael will no longer need to eat, for two reasons. First is that the replacement of his limbs with robotic arms and legs reduces the nutritional requirements of his body. Secondly, eating and human waste disposal are inefficient; a better system is required. At this time, it is believed the cyborg will need oxygen and to speak, so his lungs, voice box, and most of his esophagus are kept, but the rest of his digestive system is completely redesigned.

The stomach, intestines, and colon are replaced by a genetically engineered thinner digestive tract. Because a special nutrient solution will replace food, there is no rectum. Two newly created bladder-like organs are placed in his abdomen. One holds a twenty-day supply of the new nutrient solution his body now requires, the other holding a seven-day supply of water. The liver is kept because it detoxifies Michael's blood; so are the kidneys and urinary tract. The number of red blood cells are reduced so they can be replaced by respirocytes, artificial red blood cells made from diamonds. These cells can hold massive amounts of oxygen, allowing the unit to operate under water for up to eight hours, or even in the vacuum of space–without a spacesuit–for up to six hours. The testicles are kept to produce testosterone, ensuring Michael keeps his aggressive male nature. A new genetically engineered gland is implanted in his abdomen, designed to convince his body that he is "pregnant" by releasing the same ovarian steroids found in women in the early stages of pregnancy, thereby increasing his reaction speed.

Michael is again placed in a medically induced coma, this time for three days. While in this state, he overhears Doctor Hanchel telling a group of human engineering residents about how A.S.I.N.M. "inspired" the work they are now doing. "The Artificial Intelligence analyzed all we know about human anatomy and physiology, leading us down radical avenues of research. Our cloning program is reaching a point where we will no longer need test subjects like 487 anymore. But where we are going with this subject is so advanced that, with regular upgrades, it will be decades before it becomes obsolete."

In the final phase of his transformation, they inject molecular robots into Michael to perform the delicate procedures humans cannot. Robot viruses and bacteria build new neuropathways in his brain connecting the implanted chips and bypassing areas no longer needed—like love, empathy, kindness, and sympathy. Connections to aggression, spatial relationship, and reaction speed are improved. Memory locations for tactical experience are reinforced while other memories are bypassed. Also, nerves are grown that attach to the connections for his robotic limbs.

Other molecular robots increase immunity to disease, while some replicate themselves to provide repair capabilities that "improve" healing of physical injuries. The last thing these microscopic robots do is build a bat like radar system into Michael's sinuses.

When he awakens, Michael Andrew Stevens is gone, or so they believe. In his place is unit AA00000487. They have "upgraded" him into a Mk-9 Cyborg warrior. Still, a tiny part of Michael's mind remains his own.

When Unit AA00000487 is upgraded to Mk-14, the armor is changed. The bulky bolt-on armor is replaced by the "living" Armadillo Protection System. It encases the torso, limbs, and head of unit AA00000487 with a genetically engineered articulating plate set and helmet. The armor feeds on urine generated by the cyborg, returning clean water to the water bladder. The nutrient solution is modified so needed "food" for the armor will be in the cyborg's urine. With this modification, Unit AA00000487 can now go seven weeks without water resupply.

It is believed the W.I.D.G.E.T.S. can fight and win in any environment, even on the moon or an asteroid.

With the changes in the cyborgs, and the addition of the J.A.C.K.S. and armored robots, the American army reorganizes. Because fewer units are needed, the U.S. Army returns to the regimental system.

As Unit AA00000487 prepares for drop, Michael's thoughts again shift. It's been twenty-five years since he was "upgraded". Twenty-five years of changes, deployments, and combat ops. Twenty-five years of horror, fear, and desperation. Twenty-five years of not controlling his own body, of being trapped in a cold murdering monster. No peace, no self, no life. Not a man and not really a machine, just an *it*.

He's been there for most of it, the worst of it. The improbable end of The Forever War, both Taiwan campaigns, the Korean debacle, and the Okinawa "incident". And now, operation Iberian Cyclone, the destruction of the secessionist movement in Spain and Portugal. *I was*

And there is the human cost all this has brought on. The thousands of people killed in battle, yes, but worse, the "collateral damage". Those caught in the crossfire. Not since the dark ages has the innocent bystander been so decimated. To Michael, it seems civilians are targeted more than enemy combatants.

But there is another hidden cost, one no one suspects—the cyborgs themselves.

The early models were equipped with Zeus wire, a rapid download connection. It was used to copy the combat logs of a "dying" cyborg for tactical analysis before it completely shut down. It was during these downloads that Michael discovered there were others like him. He was connecting with these lost souls during their final moments, he felt their fear, their pain, and their desperation. So, Michael started downloading their memories in an attempt to keep them alive.

With the upgrade to Mk-16, two things changed.

First was the replacement of Zeus wire with Omni Connection. A physical connection to a "dying" cyborg was no longer necessary; Omni Connection was wireless. When the life signs of a cyborg are dropping, the system automatically connects to its chain of command, starting the tactical download. Michael learned how to ride the signal and capture the memories of those cyborgs that were like him.

Second is the newly manufactured cyborgs are all clones, and all "empty".

Michael doesn't know the physiology of clones; he's just a grunt and only needs to know the aim points, the places to shoot to ensure a kill. But the first time he "rides" Omni Connection into the brain of one of the new cyborgs that is shutting down, he finds a vast wasteland. Unit AA00000487 efficiently connects to and downloads the "tactical logs", the memory engrams with the sum of the unit's combat "experience". What Michael sees is a desolate desert with few memory locations, the DOS, BIOS and CMOS chips that have been implanted, shining like white lighted skyscrapers, and nothing else. No childhood. No riding a bicycle, no skinned knees, no mother's kisses to make it better, just fleeting glimpse from inside a gestation tube. No holding hands, no first kisses, no schooling, just vague images of sterile operating rooms. No basic training, no comradeship, just tactical engram implants. They are totally void of the human experience.

For years, their lack of anything human greatly disturbed Michael. Eventually, he decided to do something about it. Each time Unit AA00000487 connected to its platoon's elements, Michael slipped in, and implanted memories captured from "dying" cyborgs into those blank canvases. He had to be careful, ensuring the memory engrams were placed in locations of the cyborgs' brains not close to the engineered neuropathways or the locations they linked together. It didn't make them human, but at least being inside those brains was more tolerable. In a way, he felt he was keeping those that died alive.

The flight of UV-123 Locusts split up, each heading to its initial drop point. The Locusts follow an unpredictable flight pattern devised by A.S.I.N.M., making it nearly impossible for air defenses to detect and engage the drop ships. Soon Unit AA00000487's drop ship approaches its release point. The trapdoor opens, and Unit AA00000487 drops, deploying a drogue chute. As Unit AA00000487 falls away, its six CD-31C combat drones drop from the lift ship with it, flying to their preprogrammed security points. The Unit lands directly on its drop point, Mirador de le Presa de Entrepeñas. As it lands, the drogue chute releases.

Unit AA00000487 faces southeast, looking at the town of Sacedón. Michael knows the unit is evaluating whether it should fire one of its ¾ kiloton enhanced radiation warheads at the town. Michael tries to take over the system long enough for the unit to cancel the attack. He knows he has failed when the warhead streaks toward Sacedón.

As the mushroom cloud rises over the town Michael wants to scream. *Over three thousand people live there!*

Unit AA00000487 directs two other Mk-17Ds to cover the town's perimeter with non-persistent binary nerve gas, ensuring no residents will escape the carnage. Michael watches in horror as the few surviving townspeople rush into the invisible cloud of instant death.

Unit AA00000487 moves on to its next objective. The unit's six CD-31C combat drones stay within fifty meters of the cyborg, surrounding it as it "bounds" along highway N320. Soon it has Auñón in its sights. Unit AA00000487 pumps two nerve gas canisters into the center of the town. Michael cringes inside.

For over seventy hours, the devastation continues. The cyborgs of First Platoon of Dog Company dominate the environment. Spanish men and women attack again and again against overwhelming firepower. They use IEDs, they ambush, they charge the inhuman monsters before them. They die.

It's senseless, insane, but they keep fighting. Their officers rally the "yards". They are cut down. They regroup as best they can and are shot to pieces. All Michael can think is these men and women have decided it is better to die standing on their own two feet, free, than to live on their knees, slaves to the Union of European States.

By the eighty-hour mark, first platoon has killed nearly two thousand enemy combatants and an unknown number of "non-combatants". All this for the loss of one hundred and twelve CD-31C combat drones, four Mk-17Ds severely damaged, and three Mk17Ds destroyed.

As the operation winds down, Unit AA00000487 is notified to secure a location for the division's M-73A3 Heavy Assault and Command Carrier to jump to. The unit selects a location south-east of Auñón, overlooking the town. The location is at a thousand meters altitude, relatively flat, and forested on the western slope. Unit AA00000487 pulls in two other Mk-17Ds to help with security for the command carrier.

The site is ideal except for one thing; within this hill is the last undetected Spanish combat effective unit.

The Spanish had prepared this hill soon after they declared their secession from the Union of European States. Their survey of the minerals in this location showed they blocked many of the sensors used by the Americans. They tunneled out several shafts, reinforced some, and when they were finished, they had enough room to conceal a full infantry company with some support troops, over two hundred soldiers. Because the three cyborgs holding the hilltop had lost over two thirds of their CD-31C combat drones, the "yards" were able to get to the several trap doors opening to the surface undetected. Suddenly Unit AA00000487 and the two cyborgs with it were being swamped by the Spanish troops swarming out of their tunnels.

Unit AA00000487 calls the nearest four units of its platoon to reinforce them as they fight off the sudden attack. Though the cyborgs and drones rake the "yards" with devastating fire, they press their attack. Soon all the drones and both of the other cyborgs have been destroyed despite half the attackers having been killed. As unit AA00000487 awaits reinforcement, it fights off the assault.

Michael watches all the carnage with anguish. He wants to stop it, he wants to help them, he wants them to win. *If they win, if they destroy me, then at last it will be over.*

Unit AA00000487's proximity system alerts it: the combat drones for the reinforcements have arrived. They begin destroying the enemy overwhelming it. Michael sees the young Spanish woman with the explosive vest rush up to him, miraculously avoiding the cyborgs' fire. He sees the fear in her eyes, smells her sweat. Her eyes take up his whole field of vision. She grabs hold of his waist tightly, wrapping her arms completely around it. Michael and Unit AA00000487 hear the click as she depresses the plunger.

The explosion tosses the cyborg into the air like a rag doll, mangling the units' arms and legs, snapping the left leg off at the knee. Shrapnel from the vest rip through the Armadillo armor, tearing into Unit AA00000487's abdomen and chest. Michael feels the crushing pressure force the air out of his chest. Crashing back to earth, he lands in the crater formed by the explosion.

Bodies fall about Unit AA00000487 as the reinforcements arrive, mowing down the rest of the Spanish fighters. Michael watches, horrified, as the reinforcements clean out the remaining Spanish troops. Soon all is quiet.

Unit AA00000487's systems check on the damage. Once the assessment is completed, it reports to the battalion's M-70C Combat Carrier. The report is rapidly evaluated, and a new platoon leader is designated. The battalion stops communicating with unit AA00000487.

Michael can tell the unit is "terminating", even though all repair and support systems are trying to repair and reboot. It'll take time, but this is the end of Unit AA00000487. Michael grins inside. *At last, release at last.*

Forty minutes pass by. Michael hears the sound of the approaching M-73A3 Heavy Assault and Command Carrier. He listens to the change in the sound of the engines as it lands. Michael hears the troop ramp lower and two people walk down it. A woman asks, "Now what?" Before there is an answer, they move rapidly over to him.

Michael hears the woman say, "We have to help him." He turns to look at her, seeing the blond woman from his visions. It's her, right down to her uniform.

"It's just a W.I.D.G.E.T.S.; it's too damaged to save. The salvage unit will be along shortly to recover what can be reused," replies the man. Michael looks him over, recognizing he is a J.A.C.K.S.

"You're just going to kill him?"

"It's not a *him*, it's an *it*."

The woman reaches over, touching Michael's face. "You're wrong. He is a person, a real person."

As she holds his face, something incredible happens. A soft blue glow starts in her hands. It grows in intensity yet remains cool. Her eyes start to glow as well. Michael/Unit AA00000487 looks deep into her eyes. They get brighter and brighter. Michael feels he wants to be pulled into them, he feels his memories–and all the memories he has saved–being drawn into those eyes. Long invisible strings of things past rush out of his vision, meandering, looping, stretching into the depths of her radiant blue eyes.

He feels the sum of himself leaving his body, rushing through her lenses and irises, deep, deep into their depths. He's not afraid; all fear has left him. He feels he will go on. The light is brighter now, stronger. But a shadow stands in the midst of it. It coalesces, taking distinct form. Then recognition, cognizance… he knows the figure before him. "Mommy?"

Unit AA00000487 breathes its last, slumping against the young blond woman.

The Unlucky Number Four

By Erika M Szabo

Every culture has different superstitions and lucky or unlucky numbers. Finding a clover with four leaves in Germany or Hungary is considered very lucky. However, in China, the number four sounds like the word death, making the number highly unlucky.

While researching superstitions in different cultures, as usual, my imagination started working at warp speed and concocted a story that gave me goosebumps. *What if? Could this happen?*

***

Hua despised her grandfather, Hao. But when her mother called her to say that her grandfather had passed away, after a long deliberation, she decided to attend the funeral. She knew so well how her family felt about her, but deep down she hoped that with Hao's passing things would change.

When Hua walked into the funeral home, everyone stared at her with disbelief and visible disgust. She was wearing a red dress. She knew she should've chosen a black dress like her family members, but she hated the traditions her family forced her to follow throughout her childhood.

When Hua sat down next to her mother, his father angrily hissed at her, "Don't you see you're the fourth person in a row? You've always been so inconsiderate! You never cared for causing bad luck for the family."

Her mother gave her a cold stare, and her older sister, Li, quickly pulled her up and took her to the back of the temple. They hugged and then Li whispered, "Why do you have to anger everyone all the time?"

"Because I'm the cursed fourth child, remember?" she replied, bitterness in her voice. Although she was happy to see Li who always showed some degree of compassion toward her, she didn't care for the rest of her family, especially her tyrant grandfather who ruled the family with an iron fist.

***

Hua remembered how much the old man had changed after the Hungry Ghost Festival 10 years ago. In Chinese culture, the fifteenth day of the seventh month in the lunar calendar is called Ghost Day.

149

This is when ghosts and spirits, including those of deceased ancestors, come out of the lower realm to visit the living. Throughout this month, people take precautions, as the ghosts may be angry or malicious. Swimming or being alone at night is avoided to prevent encounters with enemy ghosts.

Hua sensed that something happened to her grandfather that day, and when she questioned him, he just looked at her coldly and sent her to her room. From that day on, he became cold and cruel, and even more obsessed with superstitions.

When he caught Hua admiring the full moon in the garden with her brother, the old man mercilessly beat both of them while shouting, "Never point at the moon! You bring bad luck to the family."

Another time when they listened to their father telling a funny story at dinner, Hua forgot the superstition and put her chopsticks on top of her bowl the wrong way. Her grandfather hit her face so hard that she heard the unnerving crunch of the bones in her nose. The old man screamed, "How many times do I have to tell you to never leave chopsticks vertically on the table?"

Hua's cry and bleeding nose didn't soften her parents' hearts. Their emotionless cold stare relayed their thoughts, *you deserve it!*

Hao's most significant superstition was to avoid the number four at all costs. "Our family is already cursed with you, the fourth child!" he would often shout at her. "Because of you, our family is unlucky. I wish you'd never been born!"

The only person who tried to console her during her numerous beatings was Li. "Why can't you just obey him?" she often asked. "He's obsessed with those things because he believes in them, and he wants us to be safe."

But Hua couldn't change her beliefs and rebellious nature. "I don't care what he believes in!" she yelled. "I know I'm not cursed and no matter what he says, I know that I'm not the cause of the family's bad luck. He is!"

The happiest day of the young girl's life was when she was accepted to a prestigious medical school far away from home.

***

The sisters walked up to the body to see their grandfather one more time before he was cremated. Hua took a long look at his face. "You mean old bastard!" she whispered. "I'm glad I won't see your face again."

Li breathed sharply and elbowed Hua's ribs. "You wouldn't want to disrespect the dead, particularly while his soul still wanders the Earth for the next seven days and could hurt you!"

Hua shook her head. "That's ridiculous! When you die, you're dead, and that's it."

To please her sister she prayed with her, but she didn't pray for their grandfather's soul. After finishing their prayers, they retreated to the back row of chairs. "How long are you going to stay?" Li asked. "Your room is still the way you left it the day you moved away, so you can stay there."

"What? Why don't you use the room? I told everyone in the family that I'm never coming back!" Hue exclaimed, feeling surprised.

"Well, you know exactly how Grandfather felt about you being unlucky…" Li hesitated. "He locked your room and forbade everyone to ever open the door."

Hua angrily hissed, "Don't worry, I'm never going back to that house. I booked a room at the hotel and am flying back to school tomorrow. I did what was expected of me, I paid my respects. Besides, nobody else is happy to see me, anyway."

Li reminded her to knock on the door of her hotel room as they were taught. "That way, all the ghosts will leave before you enter the room. And remember to never stay in room four or on the fourth floor in any building! I know the hotel owner is like you, he doesn't believe in traditions and superstitions," she warned.

Hua rolled her eyes and shook her head. She couldn't stand the coldness of her parents and brothers, and the lectures of her obedient sister. She gave Li a quick hug and left.

After checking in and going to her room on the fourth floor, she paused. Li's words rang in her ears. She knew it was dumb, but she knocked, counted to three, and then opened the door. Her eyes fell on the number 404 on the door. Shaking her head, she entered the room with an uneasy feeling settling deep in her chest.

Exhausted from the long flight and feeling sad and bitter from the cold shoulders of her family, Hua cried herself to sleep.

In the middle of the night, she woke up and bolted upright, suddenly awakened in a cold sweat. Directly above her hovered her dead grandfather, with that cold stare on his face, she knew so well and never wanted to see again. She rubbed her eyes, praying she was still asleep, and tried to shake off that terrible nightmare.

In an instant, his bony hands were around her neck, choking the air out of her lungs. His face contorted into an evil grin, and she knew this was no dream. Hua clutched the arms of this monstrous entity and managed to free herself.

She ran towards a door, crying out, "What do you want from me? You're dead! You can't be here." But deep down she knew, just like all her life, he could punish her even from beyond death for disrespecting his rules.

She flung open the door in terror and charged down the hallway. She hit the elevator button, but it didn't open. She darted to the emergency staircase. The floating ghostly body of her grandfather got there first and barricaded the exit door.

He grabbed Hua by the ankles and dragged her down the hallway; her nails dug into the carpet the entire way back to her room. Tears poured down her face as she screamed, hoping the commotion would wake up someone, anyone. "You've been torturing me all my life and now you want to kill me, you old bastard? How could you be here? I knocked on the hotel door before entering." Her heart froze. *Of course, this is room number four on the fourth floor!*

She knew she had broken her culture's most crucial rule of all: the unlucky number four. When her grandfather's cold, dead body dragged her through the door, she tried with all her might to resist.

She managed to grab hold of the door frame for a second before being whipped back with such force that her wrist bones snapped.

The painful irony of being a non-believer hit her hard as she glanced at the door. *Now the number four would be the last thing I would ever see?* "No!" she shouted in anger and defiance and stood up.

And then, it was over. The spirit of her grandfather disappeared as the first ray of sunshine peeked through the curtains and heard his eerie, ghostly voice, "Just because you don't believe in unlucky numbers, it doesn't mean bad luck won't find you."

Push

by David W. Thompson

Chapter One

December 21, 2011

Leona Wagner

I'm possessed, but not by an idea or desire—just the opposite. My possession is of the old-school variety palpable…haunting…demonic. An ancient unholy fiend infests my mind and torments my soul. It has stolen my family. It turned my hand against my child!

I see the horrors reflected in the shadows, and I wonder…are they real? Can my eyes be trusted? The creature controls me now, pulling my strings with the expertise of a puppet master at a county fair. My hands and mouth no longer obey my commands.

How did this happen? I am a strong woman (or was once). Not religious but spiritual at least. Why me? Why did you desert me? How did I desert myself? Diminished…sullied, my words not my own…my thoughts twisted by another…the demon. It speaks in my voice. My tongue is a liar, a cheat, and a betrayer. Do you understand? Are you listening? But no, you cannot…

It's been months since the foolish doctor read his crystal ball. He knew the demon but couldn't exorcise the beast. He sealed my fate when he spoke its name: Dementia.

***

Office of the First Sheriff

Saint Mary's County, Maryland

July 2012

Sergeant Frank James

"Frank, I've got one for you—a missing persons call. Leona Wagner, a local woman."

"Did the husband call it in?" he asked.

"Oddly enough, no. It was their young daughter." The sheriff glanced at a note clutched in his fist. "The girl's name is Naomi," he said.

"Suspicious circumstances?"

"Maybe… make the call when you get there." The sheriff handed over the wrinkled piece of paper with the address inscribed in his distinctive (and barely legible) handwriting. "Take Johnson and the two new deputies. It might take you a while."

Frank stared for a moment at the slip of paper and smiled at the sheriff's resistance to technology. Then entered the address in his cell phone's map app.

"It's the farmhouse out on Redmond Landing Road, old man Jenkins' place. A local family bought it a few years back. It's the wife who's missing."

"C'mon, Johnson," Frank yelled to his ready-to-retire, sometime partner. "Wanna play bloodhound with me?"

"Be right with you, Sergeant."

Frank waved at the two rookie deputies, and they responded with a nod and headed to the parking lot. The Sergeant and Johnson rode together in the unmarked Lincoln. It didn't take Deputy Johnson long to get chatty.

"I know the family, the wife's family anyway. She was a Nelson and they've been here forever." He adjusted the seatbelt to accommodate what he assured everyone was a well-earned girth, but jelly donuts trembled at the mention of Johnson's name. He held dominion over them. He was their king.

"So how long do you suppose they've lived here? By your standards of a qualified local, I'm guessing since the Ark and the Dove first graced our humble shores?"

"That's right, they're not part of the recent crop of imported "away-from-here" whiners."

"Like myself?" Frank smiled at their familiar joke…at least, he thought it was a joke.

"Well, I wasn't even going to mention that, partner," Johnson laughed. His belly jiggled as he lightly punched his Sergeant's arm.

"What do we know about the couple? The Wagners, right? They get along, OK? What are we walking into here?"

"I went to school with Leona's mother. She was about ten years older than me, and I went to school with her younger brother. The mother had a heart attack a few years back. Ask anybody though, all the Nelson women are lookers."

"Get your libido in check, Johnson. Do you know anything that might help?"

"They're a good family, Frank. If I remember right…yeah, my wife said Leona has the Old-Timers."

"Alzheimer's? Isn't she too young for that?"

"Yup, fifty or so. It's sad. God, I hope I never experience it. I told my kids…"

"Oh hell, Johnson, if you had it, I don't think anyone would even notice." Johnson crowed with laughter.

"So, in your capacity as president of County Gossip Central, what do you know about the husband?" Frank asked.

"Not much, he moved here with the Navy about 15 years ago. After he met Leona, he never went back to wherever he came from. Up the road somewhere if I recall correctly."

"They have any kids?"

"One boy and the girl we're supposed to meet."

"Any domestic disturbance calls out there?"

"Nothing in the computer. This is it, turn in here." Deputy Johnson's finger pointed the way. "The house is secluded. It's the only property at the end of this half-mile dirt road and dead ends at a creek off the Potomac."

The other deputies' patrol car turned in behind them as a siren shattered the morning's silence. Frank glanced at the rearview mirror.

"Good, the fire department and EMS support are here too."

"Yeah, and waking up the neighborhood."

24768 Redmond Landing Road

The winding road was devoid of any lane markings and as it came out of the final horseshoe curve, the house loomed directly ahead. The driveway was a continuation of the paved county road and was lined with centuries-old cedars and oaks. The home was a massive testament to conspicuous consumption, a throwback to the days before fuel rationing and exorbitant heating bills. A reminder of the days of live-in housekeepers and butlers. It could grace any historic street in Frank's native Savannah without embarrassment.

They parked the car in front of the columned portico.

"I guess she's our POC," Johnson nodded at a young girl just as she leaped from the tire swing at the side of the yard. The red-eyed girl was beside their car before they could climb out of the doors.

"Did you come to find Mommy?" she asked.

"We sure did. My name is Sergeant James. Is your name Naomi, Miss?"

She nodded and wiped a tear from her cheek leaving a brown smear of dirt behind.

"How do you know my name?"

"We're deputies, Naomi. We know things." Frank smiled and gave her a wink.

"Then you know where my Mommy is?"

"Well, no…not yet, but that's why we're here. Where's your Daddy, Naomi?"

"He's in the woods. Nathan is with him—Nathan's my brother. They're trying to find Mommy. Daddy asked me to call 9-1-1 and to wait for you to get here. Daddy said you'd get lost though."

"Well, right now it's your Mommy who's lost and we want to find her as soon as possible. Is there anyone here with you? Is anyone coming to get you?"

"You won't find her…" she whispered.

"Why would you say that, Naomi?" She looked up at the clouds and appeared to listen to the sound of the light breeze through the trees. She nodded and smiled.

"Daddy said his friend Kelly is coming to watch me, but I'm no baby and I don't need no BABYSITTER. Besides, I've never met her before. Mommy said to always watch out for strangers. We shouldn't trust them and never, ever go anywhere with them. Isn't that right, Deputy?"

"Yes, Naomi. Your Mommy taught you well."

"That's why I don't need a BABY-sitter."

"I understand, but your Daddy is the boss. Deputy Gerard?"

"Yes, sir," the rookie deputy replied.

"Keep an eye on our young Miss Naomi until her big-girl sitter gets here, then join up with us. We will start along the banks of the creek and work our way down to the river. We will rendezvous with you at the confluence."

"Yes, sir, Sergeant. Naomi, do you like to play any games?"

***

The woods near the water were as thick as an Amazon jungle. Virginia creeper and poison ivy wrapped around the trees and carpeted the ground. Greenbrier thorns pulled and snatched at their pant legs.

"Watch where you plant your feet, men," Johnson yelled. "Probably some copperheads in here and they don't take kindly to getting stepped on."

"Lee-Nn Wig-Nee," boomed the fireman's staticky megaphone.

"Damn, cut that thing down. I can't even tell what you're saying." Frank ordered.

"Le-o-na Wag-ner. If you hear me, please move toward my voice."

"Is that better, Sergeant?" the fireman asked.

"Much."

"Leona! Where are you?" Another voice screamed in front of them. "Leona!"

"Michael Wagner? Is that you?" Frank shouted.

"It is. Sheriff?" The voice answered as the man himself pushed his way through the vines and appeared before them.

Frank stepped forward and held out his hand.

"I'm Sergeant Frank James with the Sheriff's Department. Pleased to meet you…bad circumstances."

"A lawman named Frank James?" the man giggled.

"Yes, sir and I've heard all the jokes. What areas have you and your son covered?"

The humor left Wagner's eyes. "What about my son?"

"Naomi said you and your…"

"Oh. Oh, yes. Naomi. Is Kell…um, is the babysitter at the house?" Michael Wagner looked down and kicked at a blackened puffball mushroom sending up a cloud of dark brown spores. Without waiting for an answer, he pointed along a line in the trees to their right.

"That's where the creek cuts through. I've searched all along the north side of the creek and I'm just starting on this side. A couple of men could help through here and have the others move down to the river?"

"Sounds good. Has your wife done this before, Mr. Wagner? Disappeared like this? I know folks with dementia sometimes…"

"No. Do you think I'd leave her alone with Naomi if she did? She wouldn't be safe alone…Leona wants to die, Sergeant."

Wagner turned his back on us and headed towards the creek.

Johnson turned towards Frank and hooked his thumb toward Michael Wagner.

"What do you make of him?" he asked.

"Hard to say. People can act strangely under stress. He was put off when I asked about his son. Weird."

"I hope Nathan doesn't end up missing too."

"Sergeant James? Sir?" Deputy Gerard called.

"Over here, Deputy."

"We found something you might want to see."

Sergeant James followed Deputy Gerard to the riverbank. The Potomac was swollen, and full high tide was in. The other rookie waited on the shore with a well-worn straw hat in her gloved hands. Frank recognized the style—an Old Order Mennonite hat.

"What have you got there, Deputy Mattingly?"

"It's a Mennonite hat, Sergeant."

"I can see that all by myself, Rachel. Mind telling me the importance of it in this case?"

"Yes, sir." She placed the hat on the ground just shy of the water. "It was there, just about to float away when we saw it." She turned her head toward an attractive fortyish woman a few yards away.

"Mrs. Nelson?"

"It's Miss, Deputy."

Frank held out his hand. "Sergeant James, ma'am. I'm pleased to meet you."

The woman brushed the auburn hair from her eyes and grabbed his hand firmly. "It's Marianne, Deputy, Leona's sister."

"Miss Nelson, will you please tell the Sergeant what you told me?" Deputy Mattingly asked.

"The hat belongs to Leona, Sergeant."

Frank picked the hat up and turned it from side to side to examine it.

"How can you tell it's hers? It looks like any other Mennonite hat."

"Not exactly." She reached inside the hat and turned back the sweatband. Neatly printed with permanent marker was the name: Leona N. Wagner. "She always wore that old thing when she was running her trotline for crabs. Looks like she was planning to steam hard crabs for dinner—does that sound like a woman determined to end it all?"

"Who said anything about…"

"He will though…Michael…just you wait."

"Miss Nelson, tell him the rest." Deputy Mattingly asked.

"I don't trust Michael Wagner, Sergeant. I'll be straight up with you about that. He's a control freak. Michael keeps Leona away from her family. Her friends must be his friends first. My family was amazed when he settled here and not on the West Coast, or Mars— anywhere as far from our family as possible. Leona's become a virtual stranger to us…"

"Mrs. Nelson…"

"Again, it's Miss, Sergeant. And do make it Marianne, please. I'm not that old."

"Yes, ma'am, sorry. I don't want to get bogged down in the weeds of family politics. A woman alone and possibly disoriented is missing. We welcome you to join us in the search, but unless there's something else…"

"She was afraid of being alone with him, Sergeant. Only him at first, but lately even with Naomi."

"Please call me Frank then, Marianne. Isn't paranoia something that happens with dementia patients?"

"She said Michael was having an affair."

Chapter 2

Office of the First Sheriff

Detective Frank James

The search continued until the sun sank low over the Potomac. It continued even as the flashlights dimmed from their dying batteries. The state police joined in the hunt, providing a helicopter based at the regional airport in Hollytown, Maryland. Beams of light flooded the trees under their rotor blades and slid from side to side combing the woods. Neighbors appeared at the house and soon paraded through the woods, making the scene sound more like a neighborhood block party than a life-and-death search.

The revelations of Marianne Nelson and the location of the Wagner woman's hat weighed heavily on Sergeant James' mind. His gut twisted into knots, warning him this was more than a missing person's case. His gut was seldom wrong.

Frank had spent the rest of the day searching with Marianne, an intelligent woman who held his attention for much longer than he cared to admit. They'd laughed and shared old stories while combing the woodlands for signs of her sister. At times he almost forgot why they were there and that was unsat! He made up an excuse to leave her side, explaining that he needed to coordinate with his men but what he needed was to refocus.

He shook his head to clear his thoughts as he walked away. What was wrong with him? He wasn't an adolescent horndog with a crush. Leona Wagner deserved his undivided attention.

Shortly after 10 p.m., he'd sent the civilians home for the night. He didn't want anyone else to get lost in the dismal swamp surrounding the river. As the hours sped by, the odds of finding the woman dwindled. He feared it would soon be a job for divers and cadaver dogs.

The fire wranglers along with four fresh deputies and search and rescue hounds continued the hunt. The state boys continued crisscrossing the sky, only stopping to return to base for fuel.

Frank called in to give a full report to the Sheriff.

"Bring Michael Wagner in for questioning, Frank. Not taking any chances. This could turn out to be a murder case."

Johnson and the Sergeant returned to the house, and Frank knocked sharply on the door. Michael answered, dressed in a satin robe—already home from the search. Naomi stood behind him, her eyes wet and as big as a pair of bunker marbles.

"Mr. Wagner, we'd like you to come back to Newtowne with us. We were hoping you could clear things up for us…It won't take long, just a few questions."

"No. I'm sorry, but I have a child to look after and besides, Leona might return while I'm gone. You can ask me anything you want right here."

"Is your son back from the woods yet, Mr. Wagner? It's not safe out there at night for a young boy all alone."

Wagner's eyes squeezed into slits, and he pursed his lips. He shook his head and his eyes flickered toward Naomi.

A beautiful blonde-haired woman about thirty years old, appeared behind them. She smiled and waited to be noticed. The lines of her body were well-defined under a thin cotton summer dress. She was a vision, nice to look at like an artsy-fartsy painting or a special knick-knack your mother wouldn't let you touch as a child. Her appearance screamed high-maintenance entitlement. Frank tried to picture her paddling down a river or hiking to a distant campsite. His face split into a grin as Johnson elbowed his way through the doorway and past him.

"I'm Deputy Sam Johnson, ma'am. Pleased to meet you, Miss…?" He held out his ham-sized hand to her.

"Hello, Deputy Johnson. I'm Kelly, just Kelly. And who might you be?" She held her hand out to Frank.

"Detective Frank James, ma'am."

"Oh, now don't you two call me ma'am." She flashed her pearly whites and Frank felt her fingernail scratching against the palm of his hand. She winked and her laughter filled the room.

"I just thought of something funny, Frank. Is it OK if I call you Frank?"

"Yes, ma'am. Would you consider staying with Naomi until we return with Michael? We need him for a while."

"Why, of course, I will…she's such a sweet child…"

"No, absolutely not, I refuse." Michael declared.

Frank placed his hand on the man's shoulder, but he pulled away, twisting, and took a swing. Johnson was on him like a 'possum on roadkill. Faster than it could be told, he'd flipped the attacker over his leg and slammed his knee into the small of the man's back. Frank never saw a big man move so fast. Cuffs followed and Johnson helped Michael to his feet.

"I'm going to chock that up to the pressure you're under, Mr. Wagner. Don't mistake my small kindness for weakness or I will bring you up on assault charges. Understood?"

Handcuffed and impotent, the mean went out of him, and Michael nodded in defeat.

"Deputy Gerard will stay here in front of your home, using the megaphone periodically and standing by should Mrs. Wagner return."

Suspicion by a resentful sister-in-law was all they had on the man. The Sheriff thought it enough, at least to hold him for questioning, without charging him in a murder case.

The drive to the station was a quiet one. Michael Wagner never spoke a word and even the normally chatty Johnson had little to say. That was fine with Frank—he was never one for small talk.

At the sheriff's office, they escorted Mr. Wagner past the booking station to the interrogation room.

Frank gave Wagner thirty minutes to chill out and consider his situation. Maybe make him worry a bit. The man's irritation was evident when they watched him through the one-way glass.

"It's been a long day," Frank said. "It's time to wrap it up.

He opened the door and pulled up a chair across the table from Michael.

"Ready?"

"Where have you been? You're wasting my time. My wife is out there, and you are in here, sitting on your ass, playing games."

 "Mr. Wagner, do you know where your wife is?"

"No, I told you…"

"Is your wife alive, Mr. Wagner?"

"If she's not, it's your fault. Why am I here?"

"When did you last see your wife?"

"Yesterday afternoon. I came home for lunch. She went to bed early that night and this morning, she was gone."

"I'm told she has advanced Alzheimer's…has for years. She was cooking?"

"No, she microwaved something. She wasn't good for anything else anymore."

Frank paused and consulted his notes in the folder in front of him and made some scribbles.

"Do you resent your wife, Mr. Wagner?"

"I think we're done here."

"Were you having an affair, Mr. Wagner?"

His eyes darkened and his nostrils flared.

"Enough. I'll have my phone call to my lawyer now."

***

Frank closed the interrogation room door, turned, and ran smack into Johnson. Frank's elbow sent scalding hot coffee splashing across the hallway.

"Damn, that was the last of the pot too," Johnson said.

"Thought you called it a night already."

"I was hanging on to see if you got anything out of Wagner. From what I saw, it didn't go well. Is Mr. Wagner getting a free night's stay on the taxpayers?"

"He lawyered up fast, but I'm cutting him loose. We've got nothing and it's possible he isn't involved. People react differently in these situations."

"What do you think of him?" Johnson asked.

"I think he's a scumbag, but did he do something to his wife? I'm not so sure, but he is hiding something…"

"Maybe an affair?"

"Probably an affair."

"What did you think of the woman?"

"She's quite the distraction. I could have spent all night talking to her. Did you know she used to be a river guide on the Shenandoah?"

"Really? I never would have guessed that! High maintenance I'd guess, but I can hardly blame Wagner. She is…mmm, a temptation for sure."

"Wagner, what does he…? Oh, you mean Kelly…"

"Yeah, isn't that who we're talking about?"

"Sure…"

"Son of a gun—well. It's about time, Frank. Helen's been gone for what—three years now?"

"Four."

"I'll be damned…the confirmed loner Frank James has his nose open for Marianne Nelson, a local girl at that. About time too, because you don't have many courting days left in you."

"Courting days?" he laughed.

"Yes, sir. I warned you, didn't I? All the Nelson girls are lookers."

Frank didn't answer but walked toward the booking area and handed off the interrogation room keys to the senior Deputy on the night shift.

"Do me a favor, George?"

The deputy looked up from his phone call, placed his hand over the mouthpiece, and gave a thumbs up.

"Let him stew for a bit before you cut him loose. Also, I doubt it happens, but give me a call if his lawyer shows up in the meantime."

He nodded and hung the keys on a nail on the wall behind his chair.

"I'm heading home, Johnson. I've had enough of today."

"Right behind you."

Frank held the exit door for Johnson and headed for his car. Guess we should have a chat about all our local girls, Sergeant."

"You married your wife 6 months out of high school and now you're the expert on women?"

"Local women, Frank…they're different. Their roots are in the land and their roots sink deep in our creeks and rivers. It's bred into their DNA for so long, that they've got salt water in their veins and rich clay soil between their toes. You'll never get the county out of a Southern Maryland woman..."

"I'm not trying to… who said…"

Frank shook his head in frustration and started again. "Weren't you telling me last week about a study that said a genetic anomaly could create zombies? Forgive me if I don't take your expertise on DNA or women too seriously."

"You mind my words now. Take it slow, Frank, and don't forget to use protection."

Frank reached down, grabbed a rock, and acted like he was going to throw it at Johnson. "Go the hell home, Sam!"

Johnson jumped into his car with a laugh and slammed the door behind him. He gunned the engine and squealed tires on the pavement, grinning like a teenager as he drove by with a wave.

Frank got into his car, snapped the safety belt in place, and looked in the rearview mirror. An old guy looked back at him. Grey streaks of hair marred his temples and a five o'clock shadow glowed from the reflected silver. The eyebrow hairs, the ones Helen used to complain about, sprouted out now as if freshly fertilized. His suit was worn and wrinkled. *Jesus, Frank, are you turning in your man card?*

He needed a haircut and hadn't dated anyone besides Helen for 15 years. He knew small talk wasn't his forte, so what would they talk about? She was easy to talk to…something about the case? Maybe meet for coffee? So, the women are different here? "Maybe that's just what I need," he thought.

Chapter 3

Leona Wagner—In a Dark Place

Where am I? Black…everything black. Did the fall blind me? Yes, the fall…I remember the fall—if nothing else. The darkness filled my senses, so complete, so absolute. No features of my prison were apparent to me. And prison it was. A rectangular enclosure smelling of dank water, mold, and decay.

My body was torn and broken. The slightest movement sent pulses of torment through my spine. The fall, yes, the fall… or was it a push?

I woke in this strange bed…or not so strange. It's hard to know for sure. Is this home? I get confused; my memories are not to be trusted. No one either. They are not who they claim to be. Monsters… all monsters after me!

Sweet thoughts of family, of love, twisted into nightmarish images. My mind is no longer my own. I woke from my slumber—my skin crawling as if spiders danced on my flesh. I sat up in a bed of straw covered with a blanket on the muddy floor. Was this home? Did I belong here? I tried to force my vision to extend into the darkness, and the shadows pulsed…alive with…? No, there is nothing to see.

I feel it though. Someone or something is here with me—in the darkness. I hear its nails scraping as it moves closer…and closer still. It isn't natural, this thing…I can feel it in my bones. It is a creature of the dark, a monster of the abyss and it's been waiting for me! What does it want?

"Take your medicine, my child. Laris longs to take you into his embrace. Do not fear. It will be over soon. You'll transform, and pain will never touch you again," the voice (a woman?) said. *Her words sound like honey but taste of vinegar.*

Be brave...be brave. Don't let it/her/them see your fear! Lord Jesus protect me.

"Yea, though I walk through the shadow of death, I shall not..." *No, no more lies... I am afraid, very afraid. The sound of the creature's claws encircles me. Close now, too close. I hear its breath. I smell its stench. The hairs on my neck stand up. My body trembles and I try to back away to the corner of the rough bed.*

"Begone, demon, in the name of our Lord."

"Which of us?" It whispered.

How many devils imprison me here? The woman, this Laris demon and one who mocked me using my son's sweet voice! My dear son...begging for my help...what manner of beast...

I should run, escape this place... but they warned me—there were demons everywhere outside. The only way out was through them, or I'd know such torture as no man had felt before...the tortures of hell!

"Welcome, Prince Laris," the honey-toned voice said. "Accept our poor sacrifice."

"Yahweh, God of Abraham, defend me. Ahone, lend me your power. Jesus, the Christ ..."

"Oh please," it growled. "Do make up your mind, chosen ape of God."

The stench of rotted flesh soured its breath.

"Oh, sweet Jesus."

"Too late," it said. *Claws dug into the skin of my breast. Talon-tipped fingers slipped into my ear, and nose and caressed the demon that lurked there.*

"You want this, don't you? You prayed for this, to be made whole again."

The fingers dug in and explored. The creature's face stretched into a smile so wide I thought its blackened leathery skin might split. Its eyes shut as it moaned—a sound of orgasmic delight.

"Ahh…"

My violation and cure neared completion. One last concession to make. …Or one more sacrifice! The forgotten images, and whispered memories flooded my defiled mind. There was so much…a feast for my senses: my life, my loves, and even the bittersweet heartbreaks inundated me. I remembered it all!

"Swear on your soul, woman. You'll pay my price to be made whole? To save the child, your child?" The creature croaked, laughing.

Devils lie…Devils lie! Tears burned in rivulets down my cheek. I screamed and nodded yes. Take me!

***

Naomi Wagner

As long as Naomi was capable of writing complete sentences, she'd kept a diary. Her mother, Leona, encouraged the imaginative child to do just that.

"Books hold the knowledge of the world and the wisdom of the ages, Naomi. If you can read and write, you can do anything. The world will be your oyster."

Naomi wasn't sure if that was a good thing. She didn't like oysters. She thought they were yucky, slimy things but all the adults raved over them. Perhaps someday she'd develop the taste…like yogurt, she thought. She didn't like yogurt either. She hadn't since she was little.

With her mother missing and her father taken away, she thought of the notebook under her mattress, flipped through to a fresh page, and began to write out her thoughts:

Dear Diary,

171

My Mommy is missing. Kelly says she's worried that something bad might have happened to her. She says she's one of Daddy's best friends, but I never met her before tonight. I don't think I like her very much either, but Daddy sure does.

Daddy and Mommy were loud talking a few nights ago. Mommy kept yelling about Kelly and using words I didn't know—something about a wrecker. I think Kelly drives those big machines; you know—the ones they use to knock down houses? I thought maybe she was Daddy's girlfriend, but Daddy is married to Mommy. Mommy has a ring and everything, so I must be confused. Grown-ups can be so funny sometimes.

Daddy is in the jailhouse now, but Kelly says he will be home soon, "no body, no case" she said. Nathan said he has a secret to tell me too—when Daddy and Kelly aren't around. I'll tell you what he says when I see him though, Diary. I'll never lie to you, even when it hurts.

Signed, Naomi Wagner, 7 ½ years old.

***

Marianne Nelson

She woke early having set her alarm for an hour earlier than usual and began her daily ritual—coffee first, then a quick check of the local news on TV. Today's news featured updates on her missing sister and Michael taken in for questioning. She planned to rejoin the search and called her office to request vacation days for the remainder of the week. She planned to be on-site when the sun rose over the Potomac.

She rinsed out her coffee cup and stacked it in the dishwasher. Throwing off her robe in the bathroom, she dressed in the old jeans, flannel shirt, and hiking boots she laid out the night before.

She brushed her hair in the mirror. Good enough for a search and rescue mission, she thought. It promised to be a long day ahead.

You're not going out like that, are you?

Marianne smiled. Years after her mother passed, her voice still echoed in her mind—whispers of conversations past and arguments unsettled.

A woman should always look her best. You might see him again…you're not getting any younger.

She glanced in the mirror, applied a subtle lipstick, and pulled her hair back in a ponytail.

It looks better loose.

"I am going to find my sister today and that's all I have room to think about right now. He could be married or worse—some kind of pervert. So, chill."

You made sure he knew it was "Miss" Nelson though.

"Ugh!"

✳✳✳

When Marianne pulled up in the driveway, she saw a green church van and a police cruiser already there. A group of people gathered near the end of the lawn bordering the woods, waiting for enough light to begin their search. Marianne made her way towards them.

"Thank you all for coming. Leona has such wonderful friends and I know how grateful she will be to every one of you."

The crowd converged on her, thanking her for her words, and assuring her that Leona would be found safe and sound. Many shook her hand or touched her shoulder. Others made awkward attempts at a hug. Marianne began to sweat, feeling surrounded, corralled.

She was relieved to see the uniformed men step away from their cruiser and walk toward them.

"I think we have enough light to get started." The older Deputy said to Sergeant James, loud enough for all to hear. Marianne recalled his name was Sam Johnson from their meeting the day before, but he looked familiar from before—perhaps some family resemblance.

A young deputy hurried up the path towards them and addressed Sergeant James.

"Sir, the little girl found this in her room this morning, but she didn't know how long it had been on her dresser. You should see it." The deputy puffed out his chest with the pride of discovery, pulled the yellow-lined legal paper from his jacket pocket, and handed it over as if it were the holy grail.

Frank pulled on a pair of thin plastic gloves.

"Is this potential evidence, Deputy Gerard? Where are your gloves?"

The deputy's face flushed a brilliant red. "Yes, sir. The little girl handed it to me and I just…I didn't think about…not until after…"

"Rookie mistake, Deputy. And one I'm sure you won't make again?"

"No, sir."

Frank unfolded the paper.

Dearest Naomi,

I hope that you will find it in your heart to forgive me for what I must do today. You know (I hope you know) how much I love you and how much you mean to me and your father. He has trouble showing it sometimes, but I know he loves us.

By the time you find this note, you will know what I am talking about. You will know what I had to do.

This thing I have in my mind…this disease—it is taking me away from you, making me an empty shell. I would never hurt you…not on purpose, but sometimes it isn't you I see before me. I strike out in fear, but my heart only feels love for you. Please forgive me.

All my Love, Mommy

Frank scanned the note then reread it and held it in front of Marianne to read.

"Your thoughts, Marianne? To me, it appears to be a suicide note."

Marianne shook her head as she read. When she lifted her eyes to Frank, a single tear slipped down her cheek. She nodded her head.

"We're running out of time, Frank, if we're not already too late."

Frank turned to his partner. "Johnson, divvy up the search parties. You take a group downriver past last night's search area. Deputy Mattingly can lead the rest northeast following the creek upstream away from the river. I'll catch up as soon as I can."

Marianna ran to catch up as he made his way towards the house.

"Is there anything I should know, Sergeant James...er Frank?"

"Just a hunch, Marianne. Probably nothing. Go with Johnson. I'll catch up."

"I'd rather stick with you if that's all right?"

Frank nodded, went up the steps to the house, and knocked on the front door. A disheveled Michael Wagner answered the door, dressed in a robe with a half-filled cup of coffee in hand.

"Good morning, Sheriff," he said. "I'm surprised to see you so early this morning."

"I'm surprised to see you here as well, Mr. Wagner."

"Yes...well...I, you see...I slept hardly a wink all night...worried to death about Leona...as you can imagine, I'm sure."

"Yes, I can imagine. Do you have any recent pictures of your wife, Mr. Wagner?"

"Sure, won't you come in, Sheriff? And... oh, it's you."

Marianne smiled. "It's nice to see you too, Michael."

Michael turned his back and retrieved a family picture from the foyer table. Frank took it and glanced at the family of four: little pony-tailed Naomi, a brown-haired boy approaching puberty, and their parents. Tall, lanky Michael stood grinning with his arm around a shapely blonde-haired woman who looked as if she were about to endure torture.

"I'd also like to speak to your daughter Naomi if that's all right?"

"Naomi? Whatever for?"

"I'd like to ask her some questions about the note she gave my deputy earlier."

"I must have slept through that exchange, Sheriff. Did she write your deputy a note? The one who played with her yesterday I'd bet. How sweet."

"No, the note appears to be from your wife, Mr. Wagner."

Wagner's face flushed and he cleared his throat.

"Kelly?" He yelled. "Please bring Naomi downstairs."

"Wasn't that so nice of Kelly to spend the night," Marianne's eyes threw sparks at her brother-in-law. His nostrils flared. He opened his mouth to speak but paused when Kelly swept down the stairs, Naomi at her side. Kelly's short loosely tied robe left a lot of skin exposed and she pulled it tighter around herself when she noticed who the early visitors were.

"Good morning, Naomi. This is Sergeant James. He'd like to ask you a few questions. Is that all right?" Marianne asked.

Naomi smiled up at Sergeant James.

"I met him yesterday. He is going to find Mommy." She reached out and hugged Marianne.

"Mommy and me have missed you, Aunt Marianne."

"Me too."

"Is there somewhere we can speak to your daughter in private, Mr. Wagner?"

"Why in private, Sergeant? Doesn't a parent have to be present for questioning a minor?"

Marianne smiled.

"Not in Maryland, sir," Frank answered. "Sometimes it helps the child to be more open if a parent isn't there. And she's not suspected of any wrongdoing. It might help find your wife and that's what we all want, isn't it?"

"I suppose... Well, yes, of course. Naomi take the Sergeant and his friend to your room. Marianne, I trust you will be there to care for her?"

She nodded and they ascended the stairs.

***

Deputy Johnson

Johnson jumped back as the black snake uncurled and crawled away...inches from his feet. He slapped at the deer fly biting his neck and tried to still the racing of his heart.

"Crap, I hate snakes."

As if it heard him, the snake turned and lifted its head to stare at him. Sensing no danger or pursuit, it continued its escape.

"Deputy?" A voice yelled from the thicket to his right.

"Yeah, I'm all right...dang snake."

"Beg pardon?"

"What is it, Deputy Gerard?"

"There's something you need to see over here."

"Don't touch anything. I'm on my way."

"No, sir. I mean yes, sir."

Johnson bulled his way through the underbrush, slapping at the mosquitoes and deer flies trying to impede his progress.

Gerard stood beside a large flat-topped sandstone boulder. Johnson's mind wandered to the story of Moll Dyer, the so-called winter witch. She met her tragic fate near here on a rock just like the one Gerard stood guard over.

"Whatcha got there, Gerard?"

177

"I think it's hair and blood."

"Touch anything?"

"No."

"Let's have a look-see."

Johnson leaned over the rock to stare at the stain on the stone. Red liquid pooled on the rock's surface.

"You have evidence bags, Gerard?"

The young deputy dug into his inside jacket pocket, pulled out several bags, and handed them to Johnson.

"Nope. It's your find, you do the honors," Johnson said.

Gerard placed a clump of brown hair in one bag and took several samples of the blood-like substance.

"Do you think this is from the missing lady, sir?"

"No, Leona Wagner is a blonde."

"Maybe it was just some hunter dressed out their deer here then?"

"Not a hunter...a poacher maybe. Deer season is long gone. The hair is short. but too long for a deer. Can't take any chances though. Take the samples back to the office right away. If the Sergeant is still at the house, apprise him of the situation—in confidence. Don't advertise it to the world. Catch my meaning?"

"I understand."

"Get going then."

Chapter 6

Sergeant Frank James

Naomi and Marianne sat on the edge of the young girl's bed. Sergeant James pulled up a tiny chair that was perched behind the girl's diminutive desk. He smiled to see the doll stickers and cartoon figures decorating it.

"I think you're too big for my chair," Naomi said.

"I think you're right, young lady. I'll just sit on the floor beside you then. How's that?"

Naomi shrugged her shoulders.

"Where did you find the letter from your mom, Naomi?"

She pointed at her dresser.

"I saw it when I woke up."

"Was it there yesterday?"

"Maybe."

"Do you remember the last time you saw your mommy? Did she act like anything was wrong?"

"She didn't eat with Daddy, so I took her lunch in bed. She wasn't feeling good. She was mad at me too, but I didn't do anything wrong. She made me cry, then she started crying too. Daddy said she has the old-timers. Then she wasn't home when I went in to see her that night."

"How do you like Kelly, Naomi?" Marianne asked.

"She's OK. She's not a very good babysitter, but that's fine. I'm no baby."

"No, you're surely not. Why isn't she a good babysitter though?"

"Nathan knows... but it's a secret. He said he'd tell me later, but I don't know where he is. Is he a missing person too?"

"I think he's looking for your mommy, Naomi, but we'll keep an eye out for him. What did he tell you?"

"That he saw something in the woods...something about Kelly and Daddy but wouldn't tell me what. That night they took him to the woods with them. I was all alone, but I was fine. I saw them leave from my window, and I wasn't even scared."

"Nathan didn't say anything about what happened?"

"I didn't see him before mommy was a missing person. I wanted to tell him my secret too."

"Would you tell me your secret?" Frank asked.

"It wouldn't be a secret then, silly."

"Do you think it might help us find your mommy?"

Naomi stared at the ceiling, then smiled.

"I'll tell Auntie Marianne."

Naomi jumped from the bed and took her aunt's hand. She led her to her dresser and whispered in her ear. Pulling open the top drawer of the dresser, she pulled out a small bottle and handed it to her.

"Promise not to tell?" She asked.

"Your secret is safe with me, but can I tell Sergeant James? It might help us to find your mom."

Naomi stared at the ceiling again.

"All right," she said. She rolled her eyes toward the stairs. "Not them though."

***

Frank made it as far as Wagner's front stoop before asking:

"What was Naomi's big secret, Marianne? What's in the bottle?"

"She said her mother thought it was this medicine that was making her sick, so Naomi took it and hid it in her dresser drawer."

"We'll have it tested. I'll see if I can rustle up someone to take it in. Can I see?"

Frank unscrewed the bottle cap and sniffed. His eyebrows shot up.

"What is it, Frank?"

"I'm not sure...familiar though. As soon as I rustle up a carrier, we'll rejoin the others. Which search party shall we join?"

"The one following the river, but en route, we need to check out the area Michael claimed to have searched. There's a cliff there and the state put large rocks at the bottom to discourage erosion. If I was of a mind to... well, end it all. That's where I'd go."

"Let me make a call and then we're off then."

Deputy Gerard ran from the trees towards them.

"Sergeant James?" He yelled.

He caught up to them before they reached the cars.

"Sir, I'm headed in... we found... some...thing. Deputy Johnson..."

"Slow down, Deputy, and catch your breath. What do you think you found?"

Deputy Gerard took two deep breaths and held up the bag with two-inch brown hairs and a small vial.

"Looks like blood in this one," he said.

"Well done, Deputy. No sign of Mrs. Wagner?"

"Not yet, sir. Deputy Johnson instructed me to get these samples back to Newtowne but to check in with you first."

"Good. Wait here for a moment, Deputy. Miss Nelson has a bottle of liquid to be tested as well and I need something from the house if Wagner will cooperate."

Minutes passed as they waited. Marianne attempted to make small talk with the young deputy as he nervously shifted his weight from one foot to the other. When Frank James stepped outside, he held another evidence bag filled with loose hairs.

"Deputy, I'm entrusting you with this evidence. The hair in this bag is to be tested for DNA. It belongs to the missing woman, and don't forget—prints from off the letter."

"I'll take it straight away, sir. Um, sir? Who gets it?"

"I don't know who is in today or on call, so give it to the sheriff. Whoever gets it, I want you to ask them if any side effects from medication or plants might simulate dementia."

"Yes, sir," Gerard trotted toward his squad car and, with emergency lights flashing, gunned it toward Newtowne.

"Kids," Frank said.

"At least he didn't cut on the siren," Marianne said and the "whup-whup" of a police siren ripped through the morning's calm. They shook their heads and laughed. Marianne's cut short.

"Frank?"

"What's wrong, Marianne?"

"Those hairs? I think they belong to Naomi's brother Nathan."

***

They pushed through the marshy ground and thick brush to the point where they'd met Michael the day before.

"Which way to that cliff?" Frank asked.

"If memory serves, it's off to the left. Leona took me there a couple of times when Michael was away on business trips. There's a small cove... not sure if it's high enough to do the... deed but it's worth a look."

They spotted the opening through the trees that allowed light into what Marianne called "the jungle." The cliff was steep and dropped off without warning. Frank peered over the edge.

"Leona liked it here," Marianne said. "She loved to sit at the edge and read. She claimed that all her troubles floated away with a good book in her hands."

Frank slipped off his backpack and pulled out a length of heavy rope.

"I need to get down there. With this overhang, I can't see everything. She might have crawled back towards the bank."

"You fancy yourself a mountain climber, Frank?"

"No, but I was fair at climbing that dumb rope in High School Phys Ed class. That will have to suffice."

He tied off the rope to a stout oak and began his descent—two feet...ten feet...twenty feet.

"Are you doing all right?" Marianne called.

He waved up at her as the bald-faced hornet hit him in the cheek. Swatting at it, his grip failed. He sailed to the bottom...and the waiting rocks.

"Ouch, oh, ouch, ouch, ouch!"

He did an inventory of all his body parts. He wiggled fingers and toes and bent his arms and legs back and forth. Nothing appeared broken, although everything hurt.

"Are you OK? Anything broken?" Marianne asked from beside him.

"I don't think so...hey, how did you get down here so fast?"

"Not as fast as you." She laughed. "Guess I did better in gym class than you... plus I grabbed the thick leather gloves in your pack. What hurts?"

"Everything, along with a terminal diagnosis for my pride."

She bent down and planted a soft kiss on his cheek.

"The hornets get you?"

"Yes, you?"

"No, they were too busy trying to figure out where you went. You're lucky you were almost to the bottom."

"Oh good. I feel lucky," he laughed.

He tried to stand and winced with the effort. Marianne bent down and put his arm around her shoulders.

"I maybe sprained my ankle."

"So how do I get you back up there?" She pointed to the cliff edge.

***

Deputy Johnson

Johnson dug into his pocket to retrieve his cell phone. He glanced at the screen—a local prefix, but he did not recognize the number.

"Sheriff's Deputy Johnson, may I help you, sir or ma'am?"

"Sir, this is Deputy Gerard. I brought in the evidence like you asked."

"You called to tell me that, Gerard?"

"Yes, sir, I mean no, sir, there's more. I found some stuff online about the possible contents of the medicine bottle."

"Deputy, I have no idea what you are talking about. Please explain yourself and do so quickly. I'm leading a search party here."

"Yes, sir. You see, Sergeant James asked me to investigate medications found at the house. No results yet, of course, but I think it's bath salts."

"And you find that unusual, Deputy? That a lady would have bath salts?"

"It is when it's used as medicine, sir. I asked Doctor Hayden, and he agreed I could be right. He said bath salts can cause paranoia, delirium, violent behavior, suicidal thoughts, and hallucinations. He said that's like what dementia patients experience."

"I don't understand how this relates to our missing person case, but I'll relay the information to the Sergeant when he catches up with us. I'm sure he'll know what you're spouting off about."

"Thank you, sir.

Chapter 7

Leona

I feel my bones trying to knit back together. It doesn't hurt, in fact, it rather tickles, an itch I can't scratch. But I can breathe again! I don't have to fight to fill my lungs. They no longer feel raw hunger and need. I suck in great draughts of air that fill my lungs to bursting. I'm like a child with ice cream but shoveling in the air instead of dairy. Would my lungs ever tire of feeling full again?

Parts of my prison have come into focus. The darkness is still complete, yet I can see or sense the parameters of the enclosure. It has a stone and gravel aisle in the middle of a mud floor three paces wide. The walls are made from stacked rock and broken bricks.

I've changed in many ways like they said. My fingers grow longer. A strange thing to notice, but I have plenty of time to note such things. My nails too are growing unnaturally fast and are so strong. I would have given anything—before—to have nails such as these! I can cut meat and skin rats with them. How do I know you might ask? I must eat...and there are plenty. I can hear them...even smell them now. The holes in the walls are full of furry tasty treats. They dug tunnels into the dirt behind the walls. They visit often. The demon child...the false one they try to torture me with... reclines on a wooden bench with tied hands and feet...whining...but I know he's one of them too.

I remember so little of my life before. There was another boy, a real one—not the demon one, and a girl—Noomi?

They will come for me soon, but I begin to doubt their words. They say I'll have my revenge...retribution for the wrongs. That much I must believe...and hunger for it.

I curl up on my wooden ledge to sleep. My naps seem days long but without the sun to mark the progress of the day I cannot say.

I try to sleep, but my mouth feels odd, and my gums are sore. I run my tongue over my teeth and they're growing! Several are as sharp and pointed as knives! What manner of beast am I becoming?

I hear them now, a man and a woman. The demon Laris and the honey-voiced woman coming to take me to hell? Or is it Alzheimer's, the demon destroyer, the thief? It doesn't matter. It will be over soon. Or so I pray...

***

Sergeant Frank James

"No idea how we get back up there," Frank said. "It sure won't be the same way I came down."

185

"What's that, Frank?" She pointed at the bank and a small opening covered with brush.

"Let's find out."

Marianne held back the brush to allow Frank to hobble in first. He lit the way with his flashlight.

After a short tunnel through the bank, the walls changed.

"Dear Lord," Marianne said. "I know what this is. Leona's realtor told them there was a rumor that an underground shelter was built somewhere on the property. The former owner was a doomsday prepper, but Leona never found it."

"It's been here awhile I'd say."

"Eww...what's that? Marianne lifted her foot. Half of a disemboweled rat carcass was stuck to her boot.

"Mmm...unnn."

Frank flipped the light towards the sound.

"Nathan!" Marianne ran to her nephew and loosened the rag tied around his mouth.

"Aunt Marianne, it's mom, she's..."

"Aargh!" The woman screamed at them from the darkness.

"Leona? Is that you?"

Frank handed her the light.

"Go help her. I'll untie the boy."

"Oh, Leona, what has happened to you? You poor thing."

She brushed the matted hair from her sister's face. Leona growled "Demon!" and sank her teeth into her sister's finger.

"Ouch! Sweet Jesus, Leona, it's me—Marianne." But Leona didn't loosen her grip. Her teeth dug deeper into Marianne's flesh.

"Frank, help me!"

***

186

Deputy Johnson

"Detective Johnson? This is Marianne Nelson. Sergeant James asked me to call you. We need your help. We've found my sister and Nathan. We need help getting out of here and a doctor on call."

"Is someone hurt, Miss Nelson?'

"Frank... er, Sergeant James has a sprained ankle. My sister is having some kind of...episode. Nathan is bruised and has a nasty gash on his forehead, and I may need a tetanus shot. Otherwise, we're just peachy."

"No disrespect, Ma'am, but why didn't the Sergeant call? Is something else wrong with him?"

"He's in the shelter below the cliff. No reception there. I had to climb up. He suggests the state 'copter come for us. We're below the cliff by Whisky Creek. You know the one?"

"Yes, ma'am. I'm on it. Tell Sarge to hang in there."

***

Sergeant Frank James

24768 Redmond Landing Road

"It's been a very long day, Mr. Wagner, but I'd like for you to clear up some details—here or at the station—your call."

"I'd like to get this over with, Sergeant. I appreciate all you've done, but I'd like to get to the Nursing Center and check on my wife."

"Fine. For starters, why did you lie about your son being with you on day one? Did you kidnap him and bind him up in that shelter?"

"I didn't exactly lie, Sergeant. Whenever you asked about Nathan, Naomi was there. I didn't want her to know we allowed Nathan to go camping with his friends this weekend—not after refusing her request for a sleepover. Until now, that's where I thought he was. There's no cell reception where they were going."

"Naomi said she saw you and Helen escorting Nathan into the woods and she hadn't seen him since."

"I can respond to that, Sergeant," Kelly said. "Naomi was supposed to be asleep. We took a shortcut through the woods to where one of the other boys' parents said they'd pick him up. Not many people like driving Michael's long deserted driveway in the dark."

"Was Leona in the house when you went to bed that night, Michael?" Marianne asked.

"I... I couldn't say. She must have snuck out behind us and snatched Nathan. I can't believe it's come to this."

"Nathan told Naomi he knew a secret about you two; one he'd share with her later. Any idea what that was about?"

"No, I couldn't say," Kelly answered and looked down at the floor.

"I can," Michael said. "The night before, when the kids were in bed, Nathan saw us kiss. I felt awful about it."

"So, after having an affair and with my sister sick, you decided to let her run off and die—of starvation or worse?" Marianne asked.

"I know how you feel about me, Marianne...mostly deserved, but I'm no murderer. I admit I'm a womanizer..."

"Adulterer, you mean?"

Michael's chin dropped to his chest.

"I planned to ask for a divorce, but when Leona was diagnosed and got worse and worse...I couldn't."

Michael took his head in his hands and wept.

✳✳✳

Frank and Marianne left together.

"What do you think?"

"We have nothing to charge him with. If he had anything to do with this, we can't prove it."

"What if Leona's "medicine" does end up being bath salts as your deputy suggested?"

188

"We have hearsay evidence from an 8-year-old girl that Leona said the bottle contained her medicine. Leona certainly isn't a reliable witness."

"I guess you're right. I feel so sorry for their kids."

"They'll be fine. Kids are tough and I suspect a certain aunt of theirs will be keeping a close eye on them." Frank winked and squeezed her shoulder.

"Hey, Sergeant, you aren't married, or anything are you?"

"No, ma'am."

They walked to their cars hand in hand.

***

Kelly

24768 Redmond Landing Road

Kelly slipped to the bathroom and pulled a dried chicken foot from her purse. She pricked her finger and massaged the blood into the foot. She rubbed it between her hands, across her cheek, and over her breasts.

"Laris, Demon Prince, forgive my failure. I'm not done, dark one. I will taint another to enable your rebirth into this world. Until then, and forevermore, I am your humble servant."

Bravery Has a Price

By Erika M Szabo and Lorraine Carey

Emma Devane's heart fluttered with excitement as she and her twin brothers, Mason, and Tyler, eagerly anticipated the long weekend ahead. Their plans to go camping in the mountains had been months in the making. This was a momentous occasion for Emma—it would be her first camping trip, being sixteen years old. The twins had turned eighteen in the spring.

After a week-long of worried instructions and warnings from their parents, they were finally on their way. Mason drove the old family Jeep loaded with camping gear. It was late afternoon when they arrived at the campsite the twins had frequented in the previous two years. The air was clean and crisp, carrying the tangy scent of pine and earth. They set up the tents, gathered stones to build a fire pit, and chopped up plenty of dry wood to last all night. Soon mouthwatering aroma filled the air as the boys cooked sausages in a cast iron pan, roasted peppers, and wrapped potatoes with aluminum sheets to bury under the hot ashes to bake.

The darkness of the forest loomed around them, but the warm glow of the fire brought a sense of comfort and camaraderie. After dinner they sat close to the crackling fire, roasted marshmallows, and took turns telling spine-chilling tales, each trying to outdo the other. It was a night filled with laughter, feigned screams, and playful teasing. They made memories that would last a lifetime.

"I never knew camping could be so much fun!" Emma exclaimed. "I love it here."

Mason turned to his sister. "And you always chickened out when we asked if you wanted to come with us. Admit it — you were too scared."

"I was not!" Emma hissed shaking her head as her long blonde hair swept over her jacket. "But Mom never let me do anything because I'm a girl and I was too young. Besides, I'm a lot braver than the two of you!" She spat angrily and instantly regretted it. *Why did I have to say that? They always provoke me to say stupid things. Now they're gonna make me prove that I'm brave, which I'm not...*

As Emma suspected, Mason jumped at the chance to tease his sister, "Seriously!? Prove it."

Tyler laughed as he winked at Mason and challenged Emma. "Let's see just how brave you are. After spending the night in the dark forest when you hear animals scurrying, howling, and hooting, and you can sleep without crying to go home, we'll see who's brave."

Emma managed to fake a daring face, but the butterflies in her stomach started their crazy dance, making her a bit nauseous. *These two morons will try to scare me to death, I know it! I'm not gonna fall asleep.*

As the moon rose high in the sky, Emma's eyelids began to droop with exhaustion. She made her way over to her tent and nestled into her sleeping bag. After some nervous tossing and turning, despite her effort to stay awake, the soft rustle of leaves and the chirping sound of crickets lulled her into a peaceful slumber.

Over in the twins' tent, the boys were whispering to each other with plans to scare their sister, but the crisp, clean air caused them to grow quiet and they soon fell asleep as well.

As the night wore on and the moon reached its peak, Emma was awoken by a deep, guttural growl that echoed through the woods. Her heart raced with fear, and she scrambled out of her tent darting toward her brother's tent for safety.

She trembled as she entered their tent eager to hear if they had heard the scary sound. "Wake up, guys! I heard this eerie growling in the forest. Did you hear it too?"

Tyler opened his eyes sleepily. "I didn't hear anything. See? Told ya. You are a real girly girl!" Tyler snorted.

Mason looked up and grinned, which made her even more upset.

Realizing how upset Emma was, Mason and Tyler sheepishly assured her they'd go and check around the area to see if everything was all right.

Before they left the tent, they told Emma not to worry and that they'd be back soon. "Perhaps you heard an injured animal," Tyler surmised.

"I'm not staying here alone; I'm going with you!" Emma announced.

"No. We'll be close by and besides you're safer here in the tent," Mason assured her.

Emma curled up in Tyler's sleeping bag, her heart racing. Half an hour passed, and she didn't hear from the boys. Feeling scared and worried, she texted Mason. There was no reply and no sign of her brothers.

Emma had never been so anxious before. She had always been protected all her life. She felt as if the dense forest surrounding the campsite swallowed her, leaving her feeling vulnerable and alone. She checked her phone for any missed calls or messages, but the weak signal only taunted her with its uselessness. *Oh, why do I have to be such a fraidy cat? Okay, I might be scared of the dark, but maybe the boys are hurt and need help. Emma, you must find them! She* thought. She took a deep breath and gathered enough courage to step out of the tent, determined to find her brothers amidst the tangled trees and shadows of the forest. Every rustle of leaves and snap of twigs made her jump, but she pressed on, driven by fear and determination.

She trudged through the dark forest, feeling her heart pounding in her chest and her throat tight as she desperately searched for any sign of her brothers. The moon was hidden behind a thick blanket of clouds, leaving her surrounded by darkness, with only her flashlight slicking a narrow path to illuminate her way. Her breath came in short puffs and her palms clammy with fear, she kept pushing forward. With every step she took, the forest seemed to come alive with eerie sounds and unknown creatures lurking just beyond her line of sight.

As she made her way deeper into the woods, Emma couldn't help but curse herself for agreeing to this camping trip in the first place, but she wasn't expecting her brothers to leave her alone. She'd always been afraid of the dark and being alone in the pitch-black forest only amplified her fear.

I've got to keep going. Fear be gone! She encouraged herself as she pressed on knowing she had to find Mason and Tyler. They were more important than her fear.

Suddenly, a loud screech ripped through the silence, causing Emma to jump. She let out a terrified scream. Her heart raced even faster as she thought about all the possible dangers lurking in the woods.

But then she heard familiar waves of laughter coming from behind a nearby tree. *The twins!* She realized and relief washed over her as she ran toward them, wrapping them both in a tight hug.

"Where were you guys? I was so worried!"

"We were just pranking you… but you know what? You were scared but you still came to find us. You're very brave, even for a girl!" Mason admitted.

"I was, wasn't I?" Emma chuckled and rolled her eyes but couldn't help being grateful that they were safe.

The boys apologized to her for scaring her so much. They all decided to head back to camp and get some much-needed rest.

Emma lay in her tent reflecting on how brave she had been. She had faced one of her biggest fears head-on and came out victorious.

***

From that night on, Emma never let anyone doubt her bravery again. She had proven to herself that she was capable of facing her fear and getting out on top. She even started taking more risks and trying new things, embracing the thrill of stepping outside of her comfort zone.

Later that summer Mason and Tyler suggested they go on a hike to a nearby mountain. Emma hesitated at first, knowing it would involve trekking through dense forests and possibly facing unknown dangers. But then she remembered how she'd conquered her fear before, and she agreed.

To her surprise, as they made their way up the steep hill, they heard growls that sounded to be coming from a mountain lion from afar, Emma's heart raced with excitement. The higher they climbed, the more exhilarated she felt. When they reached the summit and looked out at the breathtaking view, she couldn't believe how good the adrenaline rush felt.

But just as they were about to head back down, a sudden storm rolled in, bringing heavy rain and winds. Emma's fear of lightning kicked in immediately as she remembered watching her grandfather being struck as a child. She froze in panic as her brothers tried to calm her. But then something inside her had shifted. She remembered how brave she had been in the forest that night on her first camping trip and knew she could overcome this fear too.

"Don't go near any tree standing alone, especially Pine and Oak! Those are the ones that usually get struck by lightning. We must lay flat on the ground until the thunder and lightning stops," Tyler warned.

When the first lightning illuminated the sky, they froze. "On-one-thousand, two-one-thousand," Mason started counting and stopped when they heard the blustering thunder. "The lightning struck about two miles away." Tyler calculated.

"We could find a Birch tree to stand under," Emma whispered. "I read it somewhere that Birch trees never get hit by lightning."

Mason huffed. "There are none on this mountain, so drop down to the ground on your belly. The next lightning strike will hit closer."

They dropped down close to each other and anxiously waited, feeling the heavy raindrops soaking their clothes to the skin.

The storm was over as quickly as it started. They still heard distant rumbles as the heavy clouds moved to the other side of the mountain.

"Let's get down to the Jeep and turn the heat on," Mason stood up and said, his teeth chattering. "I'm freezing in these wet clothes."

When they finally reached the Jeep safely, Emma couldn't help but smile from ear to ear. She had faced another one of her biggest fears head-on yet again. However, she realized that her fear disappeared as soon as her brothers told her how to avoid being struck.

***

After that day, Emma continued to challenge herself every chance she got. She bungee-jumped off a bridge, went sky diving for the first time, and even faced her fear of public speaking by giving a speech at school.

She ignored her family and her friends who disapprovingly commented on how much her attitude and appearance had changed. Her blonde hair was now cut into a short pixie style, and she only wore T-shirts and jeans. No more frilly, girly dresses.

During the next few months, Emma continued to push herself to take on more challenges. However, her friendships and relationships with her brothers had changed, and not in a good way. They seemed uninterested in the types of things she was doing. They made fun of her new hobbies and would often try to talk her out of taking daring risks. Emma didn't pay much attention to them. She was too caught up in her newfound confidence and chasing after more adrenalin rush.

While taking a hike with her brothers one Sunday afternoon Emma suggested they attempt a more challenging trail. But they scoffed at the idea, saying it wasn't worth the effort.

It was then that Emma realized how different their mindsets had become.

After that day, she started spending less time with her brothers and more time pursuing her own interests. She joined a rock climbing club at school and found a group of like-minded individuals who shared her love for adventure.

But despite making new friends and finding excitement in new activities, she was missing something. Yes, the adrenaline rush felt great, but it never lasted long. It didn't make her happy.

While scrolling social media one day Emma noticed a post from Mason stating that he and his brother were going on a trip to Europe. She threw her phone across the bed. *They didn't invite me! They hadn't even mentioned this to me.*

196

To her surprise, the boys admitted that they felt left behind by her new transformation. "You're taking crazy risks, and we don't want to be part of it," Mason said.

"And we're always worried that you're going to get hurt!" Tyler added.

Emma's irrational thinking made her realize she had outgrown her brothers. *They're jealous!* She knew it was time to move on and spend some time reflecting on her relationship with them. She thought that their fear of taking risks had held her back in the past and prevented her from truly growing as a person. But now, without their negativity weighing her down, she could fully embrace her newfound confidence and continue pushing herself out of her comfort zone.

As time went on Emma's disappointment grew as close friends became less and less supportive, they had even told her that her cocky attitude was a real turn-off. Her parents disapproved of her daring activities. They grounded her, and it worked for a while, but she picked up the habit of lying to her parents and brothers, so she didn't have to see how worried they were.

Months went by and Emma was bored and felt lonely. She decided to reach out to a new adventure group at a private school and signed up for an upcoming Wilderness Survival event by faking her mother's signature on the form.

The challenge was to spend two days alone in the wilderness without cell phones or any other communication devices. *Well, this only makes it more exciting,* she thought as she headed to her assigned spot and readied all her gear. *All alone, we can rely only on ourselves.*

Emma had been hiking for a few hours with nothing to eat and she felt a bit weary, so she stopped and pulled out a protein bar from her backpack. She scanned the area and noted how dense it was. Darkness was quickly approaching. She walked for another hour in the dark even though her body was giving her signals that she needed to rest.

Up ahead in a small clearing, she could see an old, dilapidated cabin. She walked slowly toward it to check it out.

As she got closer, she noticed it had looked empty and the door was ajar. *I wonder who lived here and why they abandoned this cabin.*

She decided it would make a perfect place to spend the night. She started a fire, made tea, and cooked dinner using ingredients from her survival pack. Stomach full and feeling cozy, soon she was zipped up snugly in her sleeping bag.

The sound of a screeching owl had woken her. *It sounds very close.* She stood up and went to peer out the window. *I've never seen an owl, I'll step outside. Maybe I can spot it.* She threw on her jacket, grabbed her flashlight, and headed out the door.

Just then she heard the yaps and howls which sounded like wolves, and they didn't seem far away. Looking around in the moonlight, Emma spotted a pack of wolves standing up on the ridge. She watched them in amazement licking each other's faces and playfully stumbling over each other making happy grunts.

Wolves travel in packs. They live in close family groups and the wolves that live alone are rejected by their families. Her adventurous mood changed to deep sadness. *I don't want to live as a lone wolf anymore. I miss my family, and I miss spending time with my brothers. Why did I have to go to such extremes to prove that I'm brave? The only thing I accomplished was to alienate my family and friends,* she thought, feeling bitter and miserable. *It's time for things to change!* she decided.

She packed up her things and in the middle of the night followed the trail back down to the starting point. The organizer was still awake, sitting in front of his tent sipping tea. "What happened? Are you okay?" he jumped up and asked Emma, with worry in his voice.

"I'm okay. It's just time to go home to my family. I've been neglecting them long enough," she said and walked to her car.

The Authors

Erika M Szabo

www.authorerikamszabo.com

Erika loves to dance to her own tunes and follow her dreams, introducing her story-writing skills and her books that are based on creative imagination with themes such as magical realism, alternate history, urban fantasy, cozy mystery, sweet romance, and supernatural stories. Her children's stories are informative, and educational, and deliver moral values in a non-preachy way.

Lorraine Carey

www.authorlorrainecarey.blogspot.com/

Lorraine Carey is not only a paranormal enthusiast but has had many unexplained events in her lifetime and has used these as a focal point in her fiction novels. As a veteran teacher, Lorraine began to write for Young Adults hoping to inspire young readers. Now residing in Florida, since retirement has given her more time to write when the spirits are willing.

Alan Zacher

www.goldenboxbooks.com/alan-zacher.html

I graduated from UCLA, studying Acting and Writing. Fifteen years after graduating from college, I returned to my hometown of St. Louis, Missouri, and began teaching English and started writing.

R. A. "Doc" Correa

www.goldenboxbooks.com/ra-doc-correa.html

A retired US Army military master parachutist retired surgical technologist and retired computer scientist. He's an award-winning poet and author. "Doc" has had poems published in multiple books and had stories published in Bookish Magazine and Your Secret Library. His first novel, Rapier, won a Book Excellence award, and was given a Reader's Favorite five-star review.

David W. Thompson

www.dthompsonwrites.com

David is a multiple award-winning author, Army veteran, and graduate of UMUC. He's a multi-genre writer, and a member of the Horror Writers' Association, and the Science Fiction & Fantasy Writers Association. When not writing, Dave enjoys family, kayaking, fishing, hiking, hunting, winemaking, and woodcarving.

Toi Thomas

www.linktr.ee/toithomas

A self-proclaimed techie and foodie, Toi Thomas enjoys cooking, animals, geek culture, and collecting vinyl records. She writes clean, adult, multi-genre fiction as well as nonfiction, and picture books. Toi actively creates for and with her fans at The ToiBox of Words blog, her YouTube channel, and on Patreon.

Contents